WE DON'T NEED ANOTHER SANTA

A BENT OAK, TEXAS NOVELLA

BIX BARROW

This book is a work of fiction. Names, places, and incidents are the product of the author's imagination or are used fictitiously. Any resemblance to actual persons, living or dead, or places or events is entirely coincidental.

AI was not used in the creation of this book or any related content or graphics.

eBook ISBN: 978-1-964616-00-1

Paperback ISBN: 978-1-964616-10-0

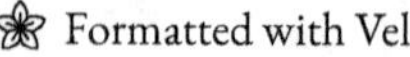

AUTHOR MISCELLANY

AUTHOR'S NOTE

If you find any typos or continuity errors in this book, please email me at bixbarrow@gmail.com. Reporting errors through Amazon does not trigger an alert to the author.

ACKNOWLEDGEMENTS

Thank you to Wicked by Design for the beautiful cover!

Lee Blair, DJ Gainer, and Beck Grey, thank you for beta reading and providing insightful feedback!

NOLAKim, thank you for your support with social media and getting my name out there!

Love, as always, to the Sparrows!

RELATED BOOKS

If you're interested in more from the Bent Oak, Texas series, please check out these titles!

Holding On to a Hero (Will, Cole, and Jason's story)

Heart Me Up (Craig and Foster's story)

Head Over Feels (Felix and Malcolm's story)

What's Santa Got to Do with It (Steve and Baz's story)

Voices Harry (Mitchell and Harry's story) – Free when you sign up for my newsletter at BixBarrow.com/Freebies!

CONTENT WARNINGS

- Discussion of alcohol and substance use disorders
- Discussion of off-page child abuse
- Off-page accidental death of a villain
- On-page manipulation and disposal of a dead body (squeamish readers should skip from when the characters park near the woods toward the end of Chapter 5 to the paragraph a page or two into Chapter 6 that starts "We were about twenty feet from the minivan…)
- A character vomits on page (see above)
- Mention of Christmas and Christmas music
- On-page depiction of minor act of domestic violence involving side characters
- Mention of estrangement from family due to homophobia
- Mention of estrangement from family due to pregnancy out of wedlock

BOOK DESCRIPTION

WE DON'T NEED ANOTHER SANTA

One retired hitman, one actor just out of rehab, and a Santa sack full of complications

Even though I don't need to pose as a third-grade teacher anymore, I stuck around to keep Seth, one of my students, and his brother Robin from being abused by their slimy stepfather. It's their lucky Christmas Eve when I find out Robin accidentally killed the jerk while protecting Seth, because who better to help them dispose of the body than a retired hitman-slash-operative?

But Santa also delivers the boys' uncle, famous actor and tabloid headliner Lucas McCord. I'm trying to decide if I can trust him with the boys' well-being—and possibly my cold, withered heart—when an ill-timed photo has the press announcing I'm Lucas' boyfriend and the key to fixing his reputation.

The skills I honed in my former life are strangely useful navigating the perils of Hollywood, but when I come face-to-face with an enemy from my past, I'll use every weapon in my arsenal to keep Lucas and the kids safe.

We Don't Need Another Santa *is a low-angst, humorous holiday romance featuring a retired hitman, an actor trying to turn his life around, two kids in need, stray dogs, an inconvenient body, barbecued brisket, and beaver onesies.*

We Don't Need Another Santa *is a novella continuing the hitman's story from* What's Santa Got to Do with It *but can be read as a standalone.*

CHAPTER 1
PHILLIP

I DO NOT CARE FOR THE TERM "HITMAN".

I have of course performed those duties in the past, but my role as an operative for certain government entities, among others, always encompassed a broader range of tasks.

However, I found myself wishing for the calm serenity of a sniper's nest as I wound my way through the crowd on the dance floor at the unattractively-named Jalapeño Holiday Hoedown. A combination market fair and music venue, the Holiday Hoedown was not a relaxing place to spend Christmas Eve.

And yet, here we were. Through a combination of luck and social connections, Cole Washburn, a retired movie star, had paid for my third-grade students and their families to attend tonight's festivities and see the band Melodious Moon in concert.

The diamond ring in my front pants pocket seemed heavier than it should. I was still stunned at having been able to acquire it at last, and here of all places.

Right now only my class and their various relatives were allowed on the dance floor. Most of the adults weren't dancing, but the children were cheerfully bouncing around with flailing arms.

Except Seth.

Seth Clements had caught my attention on my first day as a substitute teacher. Not due to his appearance or behavior—they were not unusual. He had dirty-blond hair, brown eyes, and a serious demeanor punctuated by small joking comments. He was introverted, but he seemed friendly with the other children. What made him stand out were his math skills, which were well beyond any elementary school student's.

He had brushed aside my suggestion of an advanced math program, saying his parents would not be in favor of it.

It was only after I had asked my students to write letters to Santa that I had discovered the truth. Seth's mother was dead, and his stepfather was abusing Seth's older brother, Robin. Seth himself occasionally flinched at sudden movements, so I suspected he had been abused as well.

I had paid a visit to Seth and Robin's stepfather, the distasteful Alan Shackleford, just a few days ago. In the face of my gun and knife, he had practically wet himself assuring me he would never lay a hand on either boy again.

But as I got closer to Seth and Robin, who held each other's hands tightly as they stood at the edge of the dance floor, I cursed myself for not just killing Shackleford instead of giving him a chance to rectify his behavior.

Seth had fingertip-shaped bruises on his neck.

Shackleford would die tonight.

I resisted the urge to leave immediately and take care of the chore now. It was still too early in the evening. I would not be able to easily remove the body from their apartment until well after midnight.

I positioned myself behind Seth and Robin. If they left early, I would follow. They would not be alone with Shackleford again, even if I had to reveal myself as not just a substitute teacher.

The brothers did not speak to each other, looking straight ahead at the band. Robin showed what Seth would look like in the future, with a broad forehead and a long nose. His shoulder-length hair appeared more in desperate need of a cut than styled that way intentionally. I studied their worn clothes. Both of them had grown too tall for their pants. I wondered if their shoes, ancient-looking trainers, were too small. Robin was seventeen years old and worked two jobs to pay their rent. Shackleford declined to work, though he had no medical restrictions on record.

As a teacher, I was technically required to report any suspicions of abuse to Child Protective Services. However, the foster system in Texas was not a place where Seth would thrive. Robin could be declared emancipated since he was seventeen years old, but he would not be allowed to apply for custody of Seth for almost another year. Therefore I would not allow Seth to come to the attention of the state until I had a plan in place for his care.

The boys' grandparents, their mother's parents, were still alive, but their grandfather was a fire and brimstone preacher who regularly ranted against anyone not a white cisgendered male. I did not believe that would be a good home environment for any child.

They had an uncle, the actor Lucas McCord, who was their mother's estranged brother. He had left home at the age of fifteen and changed his name. He later came out as gay, so I strongly suspected that was the reason he no longer spoke to his family.

Their mother had left home two years later, probably because she had been pregnant with Robin and unmarried. Lucas McCord would not have been aware of his nephews' existence.

However, after Seth's letter to Santa had come to light over a week ago, McCord had been informed about Robin and Seth and their unsafe situation. But he had not shown up yet.

No matter. Lucas McCord was frequently in the tabloids due to his propensity for partying and being in and out of rehab clinics. He was not a suitable guardian. It was starting to appear as if I would need to have Ripley, my longtime associate with near-magical computer skills, endow my Phillip Downs persona with a foster parent certification.

Melodious Moon wound down their final song, an obnoxiously energetic holiday tune. Two of the band members were my neighbors, and they had been more than kind about my class attending this concert, but I did not have to enjoy their music.

After politely clapping, Robin put his arm around Seth's shoulders, and they turned toward the exit. I waved a thank-you to the band, then fist-bumped any passing students as I followed.

I was completely exposed as I tailed Seth and Robin through the parking lot, but they did not look behind them. Seth had his arms crossed. The weather was near freezing, and neither boy wore a coat. Had I seen Seth in a jacket at school?

The wind blew in my direction, so once we were a good distance from the Holiday Hoedown building, I could hear their conversation.

Seth said, "Do we have enough money for one of those little red wagons?"

Robin shook his head. "That wouldn't help us get him down the stairs. We can just use a blanket. It'll be fine as long as no one sees us."

My plans for the evening changed.

"Boys," I said loudly enough they would hear me over the wind.

They spun around, and Robin put himself between me and Seth. It was a wonderful gesture, but I would need to work with him on his skills. His stance was all wrong, and he had not left himself enough room to move.

"Mr. Downs?" Seth said, peering out from behind Robin.

Robin relaxed, another mistake. I really needed to take him under my wing.

They let me approach until I was within touching distance. "I am sorry," I said, gesturing at Seth's neck. "I thought I had made it clear to your stepfather he was not to touch either of you again, but obviously he did not pay attention."

They gaped at me. Robin recovered first. "What?"

I extended my hand in the direction they had been walking. "Let us proceed to your vehicle so we can get out of the cold. Then you can tell me how you killed your stepfather."

CHAPTER 2
LUCAS

I INSPECTED THE FLOOR AND WALL THOROUGHLY before sitting down to wait. It was Christmas Eve, but from Seth's letter to Santa, the stepfather didn't sound like the type to take them to church. Surely they'd be home soon.

And if I was lucky, the kids would be by themselves. I wasn't looking forward to explaining who I was to that asshole they lived with.

I was not in a good mental state to deal with any of this, but the kids were now my only priority.

My latest stint at rehab had ended that very morning. When I'd been given my phone back, I'd only had two messages, mostly because before going in I'd blocked all my so-called friends, the ones who'd encouraged me to backslide every time I'd tried to get sober before. That would *not* be happening again.

The first message was from my agent. A little over a month ago, she'd threatened to drop me if I didn't get my life under control. She'd encouraged me to try rehab again, and I'd promised her this time would stick. Now she was telling me I was being seriously considered for a role in a big-budget superhero movie. Except the studio was concerned about my "reliability".

Hah, they weren't the only ones.

I'd texted Felicia back immediately and reminded her I'd vowed this time was going to be different. I was determined to stay sober.

The other message was from a week ago. Cole Washburn, who I hadn't spoken to in years, had asked me to call him and didn't say anything else.

Back when we were just starting out in acting, we'd met through our mutual agent. We'd both been in the closet and had hooked up a couple of times before Cole had gone on to superstardom.

I might not have been as famous as Cole, but I'd done all right. I'd had major roles on some long-running TV shows and had had a few small but critically-acclaimed film roles. A few years ago I'd even been nominated for a Best Supporting Actor award for one of them. That post-show party had been the start of my downward slide into letting booze and drugs become the most important things in my life.

But I was done with all that.

Cole lived in Texas, and it was two hours later there, so I called him first thing when I got back to my condo in Malibu. I'd be putting the place on the market as soon as I figured out where I wanted to move to. Really, anywhere outside of LA would be an improvement.

"Hey, Lucas, thanks for returning my call." Cole's voice was wary, a little angry.

"Yeah, Cole. Sorry for the delay. I just got out of rehab this morning. I didn't have my phone."

"Oh." A long pause. "Are you okay?"

I sighed. I was out of fucks to give about my pride. I needed to make new friends anyway, so it was time to be honest. "No. But I will be, eventually. I'm sure you've heard people say it before, but this time I'm going to stay sober. I've already made some changes, and I'll be starting therapy after the new year."

"That's great, Lucas. I'm happy for you. It takes a lot of courage to change your life like that." His voice was much warmer now.

"Hah, says the guy who announced he had two boyfriends on live TV," I teased.

Cole chuckled. Then he said, "Look, Lucas, I called for a reason. And I'm sorry, but it's probably going to be pretty stressful for you. Are you in a place where you can sit down?"

Oh, shit. What the fuck now?

"Um, yeah. I'm at home, and I'm sitting." Sitting with one hand clenched around the phone and the other hand gripping my leg tight enough to leave a bruise.

"Okay, so a friend of mine here in Bent Oak has a neighbor who's a third-grade teacher."

What the hell?

"Um, okay?"

"The teacher had their class write letters to Santa as an exercise."

"Yeah?"

"One of the letters pertains to you. Personally. Um, do you want me to read it to you, or do you want me to text you a picture of it?"

A letter to Santa about me? I started to get a bad feeling this had to do with my family.

"Um, can you text it? But do you mind staying on the line while I read it?"

"Of course." This time Cole's voice was gentle, as if he knew I was one thread of tension away from flying apart.

I put Cole on speaker so I could still talk to him while I read the letter. When the text notification beeped, I took a deep breath and opened the picture. It was a piece of white paper with a child's handwriting on it.

Dear whoever opens this letter,

Mr. Downs said he wasn't going to read our letters to Santa because they're private. I know Santa won't be reading them, but I hope somebody else will. My brother and I need help. I can't use a phone or computer other than at school. Alan broke Robin's phone and Robin can't afford a new one. Mrs. Frankel laughed when I asked her to contact Lucas McCord for me, but it's not a joke. Mr. Downs is nice, but I know he'll laugh too.

Robin told me not to waste my time but if I were Lucas McCord I'd want to know I had nephews that needed him.

I've almost figured out how to get around the blockers on the school computers, but I'm better at math than coding.

If you're somebody opening letters to Santa, please please email Lucas McCord the actor with this message:

Robin and Seth Clements are your sister Rachel's sons.

She died in January. Robin and Seth live with their stepfather Alan Shackleford. Robin can't go to school anymore because he has to work 2 jobs to pay the rent since Alan won't. Alan gets drunk and hits Robin. Robin's only 17 and he says Child Protection Services won't let him have custody of Seth. Please help. 1819 Farnham Way, Apt. 327, Bent Oak, Texas

Thanks,
Seth

"Fuck," I said. I dropped the phone onto the sofa next to my leg. I shut my eyes and said, "My sister's name was Rachel. Rachel Clements." And according to the letter, she was dead. Had been dead for almost a year.

Cole said, "We did confirm with the teacher that Seth's last name is Clements. He said he watched the students write the letters, so if it's a con, the kid would have to be involved in it. But he's eight years old."

"Fuck," I said again. I rubbed my face. "My family, Rachel included, kicked me out and cut me off for being gay." I gave a little half-laugh, half-sob. "I was fifteen years old."

Cole said cautiously, "She told her kids about you. Maybe she regretted it."

"I don't know. She never tried to contact me, even after I got famous. Not sure if you know this, but the reason I came out publicly was because my parents tried to blackmail me. Said they'd go to the tabloids and tell them I was gay if I didn't give them a fuckton of money."

"Shit, Lucas, I'm sorry. That's horrible."

"Yeah, they were big into physical discipline—hitting us with a belt, that sort of thing. I guess Rachel didn't know any better than to end up with someone like this Alan Shackleford asswipe. But I wish I could have helped the kids get away from him before now." I reopened the picture of Seth's letter.

"You going to come to Texas to meet them?"

"Yeah." I rubbed my face again. "I'll get the first plane out."

"You want to stay here at the ranch? Jason's mother is in the guest cottage starting tomorrow, but we have a spare bedroom." Jason was one of Cole's two partners.

I *hmmmed*. "I think I'm probably going to want to get the boys out of that apartment, so I'll see if I can find a suite at a hotel."

"Good point," he said. "Let me know if you need any help. Jason and his brother own a security company. If that Shackleford guy gives you any trouble, we can provide you with a bodyguard."

"Thanks, Cole. I really appreciate your reaching out about this. And I know my recent behavior doesn't make me seem like good uncle material, but even if Rachel and I weren't close, those kids don't deserve to be treated that way. No one does. I'll do what needs to be done so they have the best life I can give them."

"I have faith in you, Lucas. But you're not alone. I'm here if you need help, so keep in touch."

"I will. Thanks again, Cole."

After a ton of googling to see if I could find anything about Rachel online—I couldn't, not even an obituary—I searched for plane tickets to Austin, which was the closest airport to Bent Oak.

Even though it was Christmas Eve, I found a seat on a flight that landed a little after 8pm local time. I had to fly coach, but I was looking pretty rough after rehab, so with some glasses, my weight loss, and the beard I hadn't shaved in over a month, no one recognized me.

Rental cars at the airport were all booked, so I had to take an Uber to a downtown Austin rental car facility. The clerk did a double take when she saw my drivers license, but thankfully she didn't comment.

All they had left was a big eggplant-colored minivan, but since I hoped to move the boys out of the apartment this weekend —tonight if I could manage it—I was grateful for the roomy vehicle.

The holiday also meant hotel rooms were at a premium. All I'd been able to find was one room at a mid-range hotel with two queen beds. I hoped the boys wouldn't mind sharing for tonight. My gut said to just pack them up and drive back to California, but I didn't think taking two minors across state lines was a good idea until I consulted an attorney. In the morning I'd look for an Airbnb or something where we could stay a little longer.

And now it was 10:30pm and I was sitting outside the door of apartment 327. The building had probably started out relatively nice back when it was new, but the cars in the parking lot were dented and rusty, the paint on the outside of the building was peeling, and the stairwell smelled like urine.

Fortunately the hallway only smelled stale and musty. Unit 327 was two doors down from the stairwell. I could hear the sound of a television coming from one of the neighboring apartments, and people were laughing and talking loudly on a lower floor, but otherwise the building was quiet.

I pulled out my phone. I'd been using a notes app to list all the questions I had and what I needed to do. But since it was a holiday weekend, many of the items, like finding a family law attorney, would need to wait until next week.

I stood up when I heard feet on the stairs. It sounded like multiple people, but they weren't speaking.

The first to exit the stairwell was a teenage boy. He looked so much like Rachel I stopped breathing.

The boy, who had to be Robin, froze in place and put his arm out to the side to hold back a much younger boy. Seth could've been my twin at that age.

"Who the fuck are you?" Robin asked, scowling.

Seth gasped, "Lucas McCord. You came."

"I did. I'm so sorry—"

A man exited the stairwell behind the boys. I'd been expecting their stepfather to be a beer-bellied chain-smoker in a stained white tank top. I'd never pictured a stunning man in an expensive suit. He was on the short side and slim, maybe forty years old with a narrow face and sharp cheekbones that showed off his umber complexion. His hair was close-cropped but a little longer on top.

And he was glaring at me.

I stiffened my spine and lifted my chin. "Robin and Seth, I'm Lucas, your uncle. I'm sorry I wasn't aware you existed, or that your mother passed away. But now that I *am* aware, I'd like to get to know you and see if you'd be interested in coming to live with me."

Before the boys could respond, the man put a hand on each of their shoulders and said, “Well, you took your sweet time getting here. What kept you? Too many Hollywood parties to attend?”

I tilted my head. This couldn’t be the stepfather. “I’m sorry, but who are you?”

Robin’s scowl grew fiercer. “He’s our friend. Unlike you. Why don’t you go back where you came from?”

Seth pleaded, “Robin, no.” He turned toward me. “Please don’t go.”

I said, “I’m not going anywhere.” I jerked my chin toward the door to the apartment. “But maybe we could go inside to finish our discussion?”

Both Robin and Seth looked alarmed, and Seth said, “No!” Then he glanced back at the man, who patted his shoulder.

The man said, “Seth is right. It’s late. Why don’t we meet you somewhere tomorrow morning?”

I frowned at him. “You didn’t introduce yourself. Are you Alan Shackleford?”

Robin coughed, and the man chuckled and shook his head while patting Robin’s shoulder this time. “No, I am lucky enough to be someone else entirely. I am Phillip Downs, Seth’s teacher.”

What the fuck? “It’s Saturday night. Christmas Eve! Why are the boys with you? Where’s their stepfather?”

Phillip Downs nudged the boys forward so we didn’t have to raise our voices. As they neared, I could not stop staring at Robin and Seth. Family. I yearned to hug these boys close and give them the love and care they were missing. That I'd missed out on too.

For their part, Robin and Seth were also staring at me. I imagined the beard made my resemblance to their mother a little more difficult to discern.

When they were within a few feet of me, I noticed a line of bruises on Seth's neck. I sucked in a breath and pointed at my own neck. "Did Shackleford do that to you, Seth?"

Seth nodded, looking at the ground and wrapping his arms around himself. Downs put his hands on the boys' shoulders again.

I asked, "And he does that to you too, Robin?"

Robin's brown eyes were bright as he nodded too.

"Worse," Seth said. "Robin got it a lot worse than me."

"That will not happen going forward," Downs said. He sounded absolutely certain.

"You're right," I gritted out. "I'll get you boys out of here tonight."

Downs said, "You asked how I came to be here. My class was invited to attend a concert."

I jerked my eyes up to meet his, having almost forgotten the question I'd asked.

"The boys needed help with something, so I escorted them home."

I narrowed my eyes at him. "That's pretty vague."

Robin shifted, as if he was about to defend Downs. Downs' hand tightened on Robin's shoulder.

"That is all you need to know until I am certain we can trust you."

My mouth dropped open, but then I snapped it shut. Obviously I needed to win Downs over before I'd get access to Robin and Seth. "That's fair," I allowed. "I know I have a reputation in the press." I grimaced. "I might not look it right this minute, but I'm on a better path now."

Downs examined me. "Tell us why you took so long to get here. I know Cole Washburn reached out to you over a week ago."

I remembered Cole mentioning he'd spoken to Seth's teacher. I grimaced again, then looked at Robin and Seth. "I was in rehab. I can't lie; I've done drugs in the past, but I kicked those over a year ago. I hadn't been able to kick the alcohol though." I spread my hands out. "I'm sober and I'm going to stay that way. I'm making a bunch of changes to how I live my life, and when I found out about you guys this morning..." I choked up and had to take a moment to go on. "I won't let you down."

Downs' eyes bored into mine. "You got out of rehab this morning?"

I nodded.

"It seems premature to tell us you will be able to adhere to whatever changes you are planning to make."

I nodded again. "I know, but even before I checked myself in, I blocked all the toxic people in my life. I'm going to leave LA and move somewhere with a slower pace. If it takes quitting acting to keep me sober, then I'll do that too." I looked as earnestly as I could into Robin's distrustful face and Seth's hopeful one. "You two are my highest priority now, and I'll do whatever it takes to keep you safe and happy, to give you the life you should have had all along."

Robin's expression had thawed quite a bit by the time I ended my speech, but I was warmed to my toes when Seth threw himself forward into my arms.

I hugged him as tight as I could, my eyes closed against the tears that were trying to form.

"Thanks, Seth," I said hoarsely when he finally released me. I looked at Robin. "I know I'm a complete stranger, but I hope you'll at least consider giving me a chance to prove you can trust me."

Before Robin could respond, Downs said brightly, "Well, no time like the present!"

I blinked. "What?"

"For a chance to earn our trust." I noted he included himself in that statement. "You said you wanted to earn our trust. Do you mean it?"

I looked him directly in the eye. "With all my heart."

He raised one eyebrow. "What if earning our trust means doing something very, very illegal?"

CHAPTER 3
PHILLIP

"Mr. Downs!" Robin hissed. "We don't know him."

"True," I responded without breaking eye contact with Lucas McCord. "But your uncle did rush here as soon as he found out about you, and he claims he is invested in your well-being." I shrugged. "Besides, his history of drug use indicates he is willing to break the law if he deems it warranted."

Lucas took a step toward me. "I will not allow you to get these kids involved in anything related to drugs."

I had to admit I was somewhat impressed with him so far. I hoped he would stick with his sobriety. I would make time for regular check-ins to ensure his compliance.

"No drugs are involved," I assured him. "But the children and myself must deal with a certain problem before dawn, and that will require some not-so-legal activities."

Lucas put his hands on his too-lean hips. "What kind of *activities*? Seth is eight!"

I kept my expression serene. "You will not find out until you are inside the apartment, and you will not get inside the apartment until you agree to help."

Lucas glared at me, then looked at Seth and Robin. His expression turned to resolve. "Fine. I'm in."

I nodded and gestured at Robin to unlock the door to the apartment.

Shrugging, he did so.

"Stay here." I put out a hand for all of them to wait in the hallway, and I went in first, pulling the door shut behind me. Untrained and panicked children could easily mistake unconsciousness for death.

I itched to have a gun in my hand, but now was not the time. Also, Shackleford had been no match for me when he had been upright and uninjured. If he was still alive now, he would not be for long.

But the body was exactly where Robin had told me it was. Shackleford had fallen head-first into the corner of the heavy wooden coffee table. His eyes were fixed open. I was relieved to see his knees were bent. Much easier for transport in a vehicle, since rigor mortis would have already begun.

The boys had put a towel under Shackleford's head, but some blood had oozed onto the carpet. Death had been almost instantaneous.

Which was more mercy than he had deserved.

After a quick tour of the apartment to make sure there were no surprises, I went back to the door and opened it. "Come in." They filed inside. I heard Lucas gasp when he saw

Shackleford's body. "Robin, please explain to Lucas what happened. I am going to inventory your cleaning supplies."

I hoped I would not have to go shopping. Hydrogen peroxide and bleach were not typical Christmas Eve purchases, and I would be remembered.

I listened to Robin telling Lucas how he had grabbed Shackleford and shoved him away from Seth, and then Shackleford had tripped and fallen into the coffee table. They had tried to administer first aid but it had been too late.

Again I regretted not killing Shackleford when I had visited him earlier in the week. But I had still been working the op related to the diamond ring, and at the time I had thought it better for the boys to remain where they were, at least until Lucas showed up.

I had been wrong, and now Robin and Seth would have to live with the memory of more abuse followed by witnessing Shackleford's violent death. Which they both seemed to feel guilty about.

"It's not your fault, Robin," Lucas said firmly. "Or yours, Seth. Your stepfather was abusing you, and you had every right to defend yourselves." He paused. "And you didn't call the police because you, Robin, couldn't get custody of Seth yet?"

"Right." Robin sounded exhausted, and no wonder.

"Got it. Um, would it work to call them now and say we came home and found him like this?"

"No," I called from the kitchen where I had been staring blindly into the cabinet under the sink. "There will be bruising on his arm from where Robin grabbed him. It will be much better if everyone assumes he just left town. We can set up some sort of payment from you, Lucas, so it looks like he grabbed the cash and ran."

Robin said, "I have his Venmo."

And I could have Ripley hack into Shackleford's account to transfer the money to his bank as if Shackleford were alive to do it himself.

They did not have any hydrogen peroxide, bleach, or even vinegar. Dish soap and water would have to do for both the coffee table and the carpet.

"Robin and Seth? Can you please bring me the sturdiest blanket or quilt you have?" I called.

I took a small bowl of my dish soap and water mixture into the living room. Robin and Lucas were spreading a brown comforter on the floor next to Shackleford's body.

"Seth? Can you please find me a hand towel or washrag? I couldn't find anything like that in the kitchen." He nodded and trotted off toward the bathroom.

I set the bowl on the coffee table in front of the threadbare sofa. "Robin, are you and Seth okay helping us get the body to the car? You won't have to carry it, just watch for witnesses. But Lucas and I can do it by ourselves if it would be uncomfortable for you." Though I wasn't sure how much help Lucas would be, given he did not appear to be very healthy at the moment.

Robin stared down at Shackleford with his lip curled. "I'm fine. It's actually a relief to know he won't be around anymore. I don't mind doing some work to make sure he's out of our lives for good."

Seth came back in and handed me a clean but threadbare washcloth. "I'm fine too," he said stubbornly. "I want to help."

"Okay, thank you for telling me. I felt I should check in with you."

My phone chimed. I had texted Ripley from Robin's car on the way to the apartment. After some ribbing about me "working" on Christmas Eve, Ripley had promised to send me a location for a body dump.

It would be more efficient to have the children come with Lucas and me to dispose of the body, but I supposed their developing brains did not need any additional nightmare fodder.

Lucas folded his arms and regarded me suspiciously. "What about you?"

I raised one eyebrow. "You mean, am I okay dealing with a dead body?"

"Yeah. It's a little odd to me that Seth's schoolteacher just randomly decides to help out with disposing of their stepfather's body instead of calling the police like most people would do."

I smiled at him, showing all my teeth. "An excellent instinct, to be sure. But the short story is that I was not always a schoolteacher. Now, Lucas, can you please make sure the body does not have any metal items on it, or his wallet?" After another suspicious look at me, he checked and shook his head. Not surprising. Shackleford was only wearing stained sweatpants and a Texas A&M sweatshirt that had seen better days. "Okay, now Robin and Seth, please hold the comforter straight, and Lucas and I will slide the body onto it."

There was no duct tape in the apartment, so I had Seth and Robin cut strips off one edge of the comforter to secure it around the body.

Shackleford had not been a small man, and the king-sized comforter made him even bulkier.

I said, "That will not fit into Robin's car. I have an SUV, but it is about twenty minutes from here." I looked at my watch. It was almost midnight. "By the time I retrieve it and return, most people will be in bed so we can get the body to the car without being seen."

"I have a minivan," Lucas said. He shrugged. "It's all the rental place had. I think the rear seats fold up."

That would be easier certainly. "Excellent. We will put the body in the minivan and drive over to the house where my gear is stored. We will need headlamps," I told Lucas. Not to mention gloves and a gun or four. "Then, Robin and Seth, you will stay at the house while Lucas and I take the body to, ah, hide it."

Seth scowled. "We want to come too."

"That would not be safe. So no."

Seth crossed his arms, and his face took on a mulish expression. "We'll stay in the car."

I looked helplessly at Robin and Lucas.

Robin looked conflicted, but Lucas took over. "Seth, I think Mr. Downs has been more than generous helping with this situation. He hasn't asked for anything of you but this one request. I know I will feel better if you're somewhere you won't be at risk of being seen with the body."

Seth sagged, dropping his arms. He nodded. "Okay."

"Thank you," I said. "Now, can one of you boys go with Lucas and get the minivan ready? Move it close to the stairwell if you are able."

Seth perked up again. "I'll go!"

Lucas frowned at him. "Do you have a jacket? You weren't wearing one earlier."

I nodded approvingly at the question.

"I've got a hoodie. I'll go get it." He ran back toward the bedrooms and returned carrying a black hoodie I remembered seeing him wear at school. I had no doubt Lucas would quickly remedy the boys' lack of clothing.

Lucas and Seth left the apartment. I picked up the bowl of now-bloody soap mixture and took it to the kitchen. Robin trailed behind me.

"What did you use to do, before you were a teacher?"

I made a *hmmm* sound. "A variety of things, but on occasion it would be accurate to say I worked for the government."

"Like the *CIA*?" he whispered, eyes wide.

I winked. "I cannot reveal anything more."

"Whoa, that's cool."

Chuckling, I said, "What about you? Seth said you have two jobs?"

Robin made a face. "Yeah, I work nights at the grocery store and days at the diner."

I set the clean bowl to the side and rinsed the sink. "I know you dropped out of high school. Did you take the equivalency exam?"

"The GED?" He shook his head. "No, I don't have time to study for it."

I was sure Lucas would agree that Robin needed to quit his jobs and go back to school in some form. "What about college? Did you know what you wanted to study?"

Robin ducked his head and picked at a loose thread on the cuff of his shirt. "I never thought I'd get to go. Do you think... do you think Lucas would help me?"

Since there were not any towels, I dried my hands on my pants and put an arm around Robin's shoulder. "I think Lucas would love to help you go to college."

As if he had been summoned, Lucas came in the front door, grinning, with Seth giggling behind him.

"Seth's laughing," Robin said in wonder.

I hugged his shoulder a little tighter.

CHAPTER 4
LUCAS

PHILLIP, AS HE'D ASKED ME TO CALL HIM, SUGGESTED we'd have a better chance of getting the body downstairs without anyone seeing us if we waited another hour. To kill the time, he told Seth and Robin to pack up their belongings.

Phillip looked through Shackleford's wallet, and I sat on the couch while we waited. I was shocked at how calm I felt about dealing with a dead body. I knew I was tired, and it helped that Phillip had treated the whole thing so matter-of-factly, like it was a complicated household chore instead of a gruesome felony. Everything would probably hit me later. I stifled a chuckle as I imagined telling the therapist at rehab about all this. I guessed I would have to vent about it to Phillip instead, and he did not strike me as a warm and empathetic person.

Though he'd been great with Seth and Robin.

Phillip said, "You just got to town, so it would make sense that Seth and Robin go stay with you. That way you can all say you last saw Shackleford tonight, and he will have taken off when you return to the apartment."

I nodded. "I'll call him from my phone a couple of times next week to make it look like I want to talk to him about giving up his parental rights."

Phillip stilled. "Shackleford did not have any parental rights. Your sister never married him. The boys stayed with him after your sister passed away only because no one asked about them." He made a face. "And Shackleford wanted Robin to pay the rent."

Well, if that was true it would make the legalities of everything much easier. "Are you sure? Did the kids tell you that?"

Phillip looked at me like I was a small child who'd said something cute. "I had a friend perform background checks on you and your sister to make sure you were really related."

"Oh." I didn't know how to feel about that. "That's, um, kind of you to look out for the boys, but...." I spread my hands out, unable to articulate the various emotions running through me.

He raised one eyebrow and smirked. "But you are offended I stepped in when it was none of my business? You feel like your privacy was violated? You wonder if I run background checks on everyone I meet?"

I spluttered a laugh. "Pretty much all of those. Sorry."

He smiled kindly. "I understand. You have every right to those feelings." Then his face turned stone cold. "But, Lucas, I did that for Seth and Robin. If I can use my contacts and skills from my old life to make sure they are protected, I will do it. No matter who gets offended or irritated."

His eyes flashed with determination at the end of that little speech. For the first time in forever, I felt a stirring of attraction. Interesting. I'd had a decided lack of sex drive for months now. In rehab my therapist and I argued over whether it was due to the alcohol or because of some sort of depression I'd supposedly been trying to mask with the alcohol. But I didn't feel depressed, and my dick was thinking about saying hello, so maybe I had an answer.

"I feel the same," I told him. "Not the skills part. Lord knows I don't have many of those outside of acting. But that Seth and Robin are the important thing here."

We stared at each other, both of us smiling while we sat next to a dead body, until Robin called out to see if they could take their mother's photo albums from Shackleford's room.

Phillip went to help them, muttering something about wishing he'd brought gloves.

When he came back, I had my payment app open. "I'm taking your suggestion and sending Shackleford some money. Especially since he didn't have any parental rights, it wouldn't look odd for me to *reimburse* him—" I made air quotes "—for his childcare expenses." I'd never get the money back, but the peace of mind would be more than worth it. I wrote, *Thank you for taking care of Robin and Seth* in the note field for the transaction.

Phillip leaned over my shoulder to look at what I was typing. I tried to ignore the woodsy scent of his body wash. When *was* the last time I'd gotten laid? Ugh, it'd been almost a year.

And now I was attracted to a schoolteacher in a suit who may or may not have had a past profession involving dead bodies.

The fact that he was gorgeous and confident, everything I wasn't these days, had very little to do with it.

Right.

I wanted a drink. I'd seen some bottles in the trash in the kitchen, but I took a deep breath instead of going to look for any unopened ones.

Robin and Seth came into the living room with a couple of ratty backpacks, one duffle bag, and two garbage sacks. That was everything they owned? I tried to pretend my heart wasn't hurting for the way they'd been living. I could've helped if I'd only known.

"What if we forgot something?" Seth asked.

Phillip pocketed Shackleford's phone and wallet before picking up the garbage sacks. "Not to worry. I will come back tomorrow or the next day to make it look like he packed up and drove away. I can get anything you left behind then."

Seth nodded, reassured.

We all went together to take the boys' things to the minivan, everyone keeping an eye out for neighbors or other passersby. We saw no one, and all the windows overlooking the parking lot were dark.

Phillip stationed Robin at the bottom of the stairs and Seth on the second-floor landing, telling them if they saw any people, they were to call out to each other as if they'd forgotten something.

Shackleford was heavier than I'd expected. I'd seen his body, of course, but I hadn't been to the gym since my TV show wrapped in October. In rehab I'd done cardio almost exclusively. My muscles weren't prepared to carry the lower half of a 250-pound man down two flights of stairs.

And the fact that I had to put my hands under his knees, which were locked in a bent position by the rigor mortis, was distractingly nauseating.

Phillip, even though he was smaller than I was, had no problem lifting Shackleford's shoulders. He even went down the stairs first.

By the time we reached the parking lot, I was puffing like I'd just run a marathon, and my shirt was sticking to my back and chest. The boys had headed for the parking lot as soon as they'd seen us on the stairs, so when we got to ground level Robin jumped in and took the legs from me.

"Sorry," I said between pants, "I'm out of shape." I tore my jacket off to try to cool down.

Phillip scoffed, "You are healing. You did very well given what your body went through in rehab."

Why that small bit of praise made my throat tighten, I couldn't have said.

Seth opened the back hatch of the minivan, and Phillip and Robin placed Shackleford's body in the rear cargo area alongside my suitcase. Earlier Seth and I had moved the third row of seats forward, so there was plenty of room for Seth and Robin's meager belongings as well.

Once the doors were shut, no one could tell what we were transporting.

"Ah, splendid," Phillip said, holding up his phone. "My friend has sent me the location of an area about an hour southwest of here that will be perfect for, ah, hiding the body."

He opened the driver's side door and got behind the wheel.

"Hey, wait a minute!"

"Yes?" Phillip stuck the key in the ignition. Where had he gotten the key? I patted my empty front pocket.

"Uh, I'm supposed to be the only driver according to the rental contract."

I got the *isn't-the-small-child-adorable* expression again.

"I know where we are going, and you need to conserve your energy. You have had a long day, even before the exertion of carrying that weight down the stairs."

"Fine," I huffed before stomping around to the passenger side.

Seth and Robin had already belted themselves in by the time I got into the front seat. Both of them were looking around the minivan, not at me.

Phillip turned on the radio. Tina Turner was singing about not needing another hero. I looked at Phillip. He'd been the hero to the boys tonight. I hoped I would be their hero one day too.

"Can we listen to Christmas music?" Seth asked.

Phillip flipped the channel but got only static.

"Sorry," I said. "It didn't come with satellite radio."

Robin said, "There's only one FM station that comes in around here. If you leave town, you can get stations from Austin or San Antonio."

But to Seth's delight the next song on the local station was Bob and Doug McKenzie's version of "The 12 Days of Christmas".

"We'll be there in about fifteen minutes. You should rest," Phillip told me quietly underneath Seth and Robin shouting "Hoser!" at each other.

I thought about protesting that the time difference meant it didn't seem as late to me as the clock said it was. I thought about telling him I'd slept on the flight.

Instead I nodded and leaned my seat back a little so I could close my eyes.

I didn't hear the next song.

CHAPTER 5
PHILLIP

When we reached the house that used to belong to my friends George and Katrina, I parked the minivan in the driveway next to the SUV I kept here and whispered to the boys to let Lucas sleep.

This SUV was not the one that Phillip Downs, mild-mannered third-grade teacher, drove to work at the elementary school. This SUV was used for my more illicit activities, such as the one Lucas and I would be embarking on tonight.

However, even though it would be much better off-road than the minivan, we could not move the body from one vehicle to the other in the open on the driveway. The garage was already full of George and Katrina's cars and moving those would take too long.

Well, if the minivan was damaged, I would purchase it from the rental agency. Lucas would need something practical to drive the boys around in anyway.

Robin and Seth helped me carry their belongings and Lucas' suitcase into the house.

I shut the door behind us and addressed them. "This house belonged to my friends George and Katrina. They left it to me after they passed away a few months ago." Robin made a small sound, and Seth just looked at me wide-eyed. "I need to be sure you will be comfortable staying here by yourselves for a few hours."

Robin shot a glance at his brother, then said, "Uh, do you live here?"

I shook my head. "Not at the moment, but I will stay with you while you are here."

"Where do you live?" Seth asked.

I gave him a small smile. "I have a one-bedroom apartment I have been living in while I settled George and Katrina's estate." Then I said, "I did purchase a new bed for the primary bedroom here. Could you please see if you can find some sheets for it? And there are two guest bedrooms. You can each pick the one you like." I wrinkled my nose. "I am not sure when those sheets were last washed, however, so if they are dusty you will need to change them."

They nodded, looking around at what they could see of the living room and kitchen. The lines of the house were contemporary, but George and Katrina had preferred heavy, traditional-style furniture. It would hold up well to two boys using it.

"And I am sorry but there is not any fresh food in the refrigerator. However, I believe there are some snacks and sodas. You can help yourself to whatever you can find." Lucas could make rules for them later on. Right now, I just needed the boys to stay calm. "We can go out for breakfast in the morning."

"Got it," Robin said. "Can we watch TV?"

I nodded. "I am not sure if the cable or streaming services are still active, but please take advantage of whatever is available."

"Thanks," he said.

"Okay. I need to get some different clothes out of my SUV." I gestured at my suit. "Go pick out rooms for yourselves and I will be right back."

They took off to explore, and I went back outside. Lucas was still asleep in the minivan, looking much younger than his 34 years, even with the scruffy beard. I admired his fortitude tonight. I hoped he would allow me to stay publicly present in the boys' lives. I thought I would enjoy getting to know Lucas as well.

I lifted open the SUV's hatch and pulled out my backpack. After a quick look around, I unlocked the inside storage compartment and removed the duffel bag that held the most practical of my weapons. George had a gun safe in the house, but none of his arsenal had been cleaned or fired since his death two months ago.

I shut the SUV's hatch and returned to the house.

The boys were in one of the guest bedrooms, chattering while unpacking some of their belongings. They had put Lucas' suitcase in the primary bedroom. I went inside and shut the door so I could change clothes.

I hung my suit and shirt in the closet. They were a little worse for wear, but I was not sure I would have time to go by my apartment in the morning to get fresh clothes. I had donated all of George and Katrina's things last month, so the closet was empty except for my suit and shirt.

I looked at the diamond ring that had been in the pocket of my suit pants. George and Katrina had died because of it. I had avenged their deaths, but it had taken me until tonight to recover the ring. How I would get rid of it was a problem for another day.

There was a safe in George's study, but I did not want the boys to see it. I went to the back of the closet and opened George's gun safe. The ring could stay in there for now.

I pulled on my tactical pants, black t-shirt, and boots. Then I added holsters for two guns and a knife before donning a jacket.

I put my remaining weapons in the gun safe, then closed and locked it.

Picking up my backpack, I exited the primary bedroom. I ran into Robin in the hallway. He was holding a stack of bed linens.

"Do you think these will fit the new bed in there?" he asked.

I shrugged. "If they do not, no need to worry. Your Uncle Lucas will be fine with just a blanket for tonight and I will sleep on the sofa."

"Okay. Are you leaving now?"

"I need to get some items from the garage, but then we will be on our way."

"Can we look in the garage too?" Seth said from behind Robin.

"Of course. Robin, set those sheets down for now and both of you can help me."

They followed me into the climate-controlled garage. I led them past George's pricey Maserati and Katrina's slightly less ostentatious Porsche SUV.

I made a mental note to dispose of Alan Shackleford's car the next day. That had been the vehicle Robin had driven to the Holiday Hoedown, so he would need another car.

"Robin," I said. "If there is an emergency, the keys to these cars are in the first drawer in the kitchen. My SUV is parked behind the sports car, but you should be able to back out the Porsche without a problem." I could not give Robin the keys to my SUV, given the additional weaponry still in the back.

Robin stiffened. "Um, okay." His eyes darted between me and the cars. "I... Those look expensive."

"Only if there is an emergency," I said patiently. "We should only be gone a few hours."

On the far side of the garage was a large metal cabinet. I opened the doors to the top half, and Robin and Seth made *Ooooh* sounds.

This was where George had kept his *just in case* supplies. Everything from zip ties to bungee cords, to burner phones and tracking devices.

"Seth, please make sure these work." I handed him two headlamps and two small flashlights.

While he turned those on, I passed Robin a burner phone. "Plug this in when we get back inside. I will put my number in it for you. This phone is just for now. We will get you a better one soon."

Or Lucas would. I felt a pang of disappointment that I would not be needed much longer. Which was irrational and therefore irritating.

Robin gulped and nodded.

The headlamps and flashlights worked, so I put them in my backpack along with a coil of rope, four heavy-duty garbage bags, some alcohol wipes, and two pairs of leather gloves.

Then I ushered Robin and Seth back into the house. Robin unboxed the phone and plugged it in while I took four bottles of water out of the refrigerator and dropped them in my backpack.

We entered my number in the phone and tested that it worked. I told them, "I will have Lucas text you from the road so you have his number as well."

They nodded. Seth asked, "Is Uncle Lucas okay? He didn't look too good after taking Alan's body down the stairs. And now he's sleeping."

I set my pack down on the counter and turned to face Seth. "Your Uncle Lucas has been sick for a while, but he is getting better now. You remember he told you about going to rehab? That was so he could stop drinking. His body is still getting over having that poison in his system, so he is going to need some time before he is strong again."

Seth chewed on his lip some more. "Oh."

I said, "I am sure you will have questions, and your Uncle Lucas will answer them for you."

Robin put his arm around Seth. "We'll help Uncle Lucas." He looked significantly at me. "And we have Phillip's phone number now in case Uncle Lucas, uh, gets sick again."

I gave him a sharp nod. "Any time, day or night."

I picked up my pack.

"Um," Robin said. "I'm supposed to work at the diner

starting at 11am. Then I have a shift at the grocery store overnight. What do I do if you're not back?"

"Do you like either of those jobs?"

"Well, no, but—"

"Do you feel any loyalty to the management at either business?"

Robin made a face. "No, but the rent...."

I put my hand up. "Robin. The lease is not in your name. Alan was legally responsible for the rent. And after this weekend, Alan's car will be gone, his belongings will be gone, and you and Seth are already gone. The landlord cannot come after you for the rent since you are minors and not on the lease." I looked him in the eye. "Quit your jobs. Do not worry about giving any notice. They will be fine without you. Lucas will make sure you have a place to stay and everything else you need." I gave him a wicked smile. "Or he will answer to me."

Robin tentatively smiled back. "Okay. Um, thanks."

I squeezed his shoulder. "You boys get some rest. If you do not want to sleep, you can look around anywhere in the house that is not locked. I believe there is a game console somewhere."

Robin's face lit up. "Alright!"

Seth, however, was not acting excited. His eyes were wide and he chewed on his lower lip.

I released Robin and knelt down. "Seth, did you need something before I go?"

He seemed to be trying to decide what to say, then he burst out with, "Can I hug you?"

My heart made a strange fluttering thump. "Of course." I opened my arms for him, then I tugged on Robin's sleeve until he leaned over to join the hug as well.

"Merry Christmas, you two," I said.

They chorused, "Merry Christmas," back to me.

Lucas slept for another hour.

I had been concerned about him helping me carry Shackleford down the stairs, but I could not have done it on my own. I would do my best to make sure Lucas conserved his energy going forward. At least until his body recovered from the toll his alcoholism and the withdrawal had taken.

Assuming I was still in touch with him by that time. I planned to ensure Seth and Robin were settled and happy, though I did not have to go through Lucas to do that.

But I wanted to.

Before we met, I had expected Lucas to be a carefree, thoughtless pleasure-seeker who would consider Seth and Robin an inconvenience.

The man I had met tonight had been so much more. Lucas cared about the boys. He tried not to show it, but he was appalled at the way they had been living. He and his sister might not have been on good terms, but I could tell Lucas would have stepped in to help his nephews if he had been aware of their need.

I glanced over at him. The lights of the highway emphasized his hollowed cheeks and sunken eyes. He had mentioned moving out of LA. Smart of him to get away from the parties and the temptations. Perhaps he would move here to Bent Oak and keep the boys in a familiar town.

Perhaps Lucas needed Seth and Robin just as much as they needed him. The boys would give him a purpose, something to focus on, a reason not to slide back into his drinking and drug use.

They would be a family.

And it was time I decided where *I* wanted to move next. After I fulfilled my substitute teaching commitment, I would not be able to tolerate returning to the home renovation project I had started several months ago after I retired.

When I had bought the house, an ill-kempt Victorian in a northern California coastal town, I had thought the manual labor would be relaxing after so many years of risking my life on a daily basis.

I had been wrong.

It had not taken long for me to understand I craved more mental stimulation than listening to an audiobook while I watched paint dry. Literally.

These past weeks, working as a substitute teacher, watching the children's eyes light up as they grasped new concepts, making friends with my neighbors, and now helping Seth and Robin, had helped me recognize I needed more in my life than a project.

I needed people. Just like Lucas did. Mine would have to be a found family instead of blood, but I had at least proven I was capable of creating new friendships.

I exited the highway and turned into the parking lot of Buc-ee's, an enormous 24-hour convenience store, and the lights shining through the windshield woke Lucas.

He jerked in his seat and sat up. "Wha...?" He rubbed his face. "Where are we?"

"About halfway between Austin and San Antonio. I thought you might appreciate some coffee before we take care of our task."

I pulled into a parking spot. The place was surprisingly busy, given its remoteness and that it was Christmas Eve.

Lucas rubbed his face again. "Is that a giant beaver statue?"

I smiled. "You are not in Hollywood anymore, Lucas."

Which reminded me. I reached behind my seat for my backpack and pulled out a black baseball cap.

"Here. It is better than nothing for a disguise." Given Lucas' pallor, scruffy beard, and gauntness, I did not think it likely he would be recognized, but assumptions like that could get someone killed, so I preferred to err on the side of caution.

I took some cash from my wallet and handed it to Lucas. "In case you wish to purchase something."

His eyes went wide with understanding. "No credit card trail. Got it."

Inside, I was astounded by the array of goods the store offered. Everything from hunting equipment to decorative pillows to candy bars were on display. The smell of barbecued meat permeated the entire building. While Lucas went to find the restroom, I filled a shopping basket with food items we could take back to George and Katrina's house—*the* house—with us.

The cashier, whose nametag read "Darla", graciously allowed me to leave my basket at the checkout counter and helpfully pointed out several sizes of coolers. I chose one and when Lucas caught up to me I had filled it with cheeses, five pounds of chopped barbecued brisket in sauce, some breakfast pastries called kolaches, and fresh fruit.

Lucas whistled. "Damn, this place has everything."

He filled two coffee cups for us. I took mine with just a bit of cream, but Lucas liked an inordinate amount of sugar in his.

"Can you think of anything else we need?" I asked. We had been in the store longer than I was comfortable with at that point.

He looked around, then pointed at me. "It's Christmas."

I cocked my head. "Yes?"

He whacked the back of his hand on my chest. "Come on. We need to get presents."

For Seth and Robin. Of course. Lucas had good parental instincts. He was the right choice to be the boys' guardian.

I parked my cooler with Darla and told her ruefully I would be right back.

"Take your time, sugar," she said. "I've got all night."

It was past 2am. I would give Lucas ten minutes to shop.

When I found him, his coffee was gone and he had a shopping basket full of holiday candy, honeyed pecans, two board games, four matching t-shirts, and four wadded-up *somethings* made out of brown and red plush fabric.

We were near the clothing, and since neither boy had a decent coat, I guessed sizes and got them each a zip-up fleece jacket with a hood and an unfortunate cartoon beaver on the chest. Needs must and all that.

We took our purchases to the register, where I unloaded everything onto the counter. Lucas, however, took his basket of gifts over to a different register.

"Looks like y'all'll be havin' a fun Christmas mornin'," Darla observed. "Y'all'll want some Beaver Nuggets, especially if there'll be kids." She pointed at a display next to the register, which boasted several flavors of "Beaver Nuggets". They were puffy candies that appeared to be made almost wholly from corn syrup and sugar. I was certain the boys would love them, so I threw in a couple of flavors I chose at random.

I wondered how long it had been since Seth and Robin had been to the dentist.

Darla also helpfully told me she was charging me for a bag of ice for the cooler and where to find the freezer outside as we left.

Lucas appeared at my elbow with his shopping bags. Once I had paid, we wished Darla a merry Christmas and hauled our purchases outside. Lucas helped me put everything in the second row of seats in the minivan, and he volunteered to jog back to get the bag of ice from the huge freezer by the doors.

Once we had organized most of the food in the cooler and settled into our seats, it was 2:45am. We still had enough time, but it would be close.

As I pulled out of the parking space, Lucas shook his head. "If the people in there only knew we had a body in the back of the minivan. I bet that's never happened here before."

I made a noncommittal noise. This store was fairly close to the town of Wimberly. I had heard rumors about a mercenary group based there, so I would not take Lucas' bet.

We were back on the highway before Lucas asked the question I had been waiting for.

"So what's the plan for the body?"

"My friend sent me the coordinates of some land with a large colony of feral hogs on it."

Lucas sucked in a breath. "Okay, yeah. I've heard pigs will eat, uh, dead people. And those are scary motherfuckers. I've seen them from the car outside Los Angeles a few times." He hesitated, then asked, "Does your friend know why you need to find feral hogs in the middle of the night on Christmas Eve?"

"He does. Like myself, he also used to be in a different line of work."

Lucas did not ask any more questions.

Twenty minutes later we left the highway far behind and I turned off a one-lane gravel road onto a barely-there dirt track. The minivan's suspension could not keep up with the ruts, and the jarring thuds were louder than I would have liked.

I wished I could turn off the headlights in case anyone was looking in our direction, but we would never be able to follow the road, such as it was, if I did.

At a certain point the navigation app told me we had arrived. The map on my phone showed some sort of creek about a hundred yards to the west of the road. Between the minivan and the creek was a thick swath of trees. Trees hopefully full of feral hogs.

I stopped the car and shut off the headlights. I had already made sure the interior lights were off.

I pulled out my backpack and handed Lucas one of the headlamps and a flashlight. "We will take the body a few yards into the trees."

"Okay."

We got out of the minivan. I pulled the shopping bag I had set aside out of the back seat and put my arm through the handles.

"What's that?" Lucas asked.

I grinned at him. "Bait."

We opened the rear hatch.

I said, "Lucas, are you feeling well enough to do this? I can drag the body if not."

Lucas shook his head, rubbing his arms against the cold. "I'm good."

I wished I had thought to purchase a heavier jacket for Lucas when I had bought them for Seth and Robin.

"Be careful," I told him. "Feral hogs can weigh up to 500 pounds. They will attack humans if provoked, so if we hear movement in the trees, we drop the body and run back to the car."

"Got it."

The ground was just as uneven off the dirt road as on it. If neither of us ended up with a twisted ankle, it would be a Christmas miracle.

Shackleford had not become any lighter, and the rutted ground was much more difficult to navigate while carrying him than the apartment stairs had been. Lucas began to breathe heavily even before we got to the trees.

"Stop," I said "Put him down." We dropped the body unceremoniously to the ground. "If we unwrap him, we can drag him on the comforter over the grass."

Lucas nodded. "Let's try it."

I used my knife to cut the bindings around the body, and we unwrapped the comforter. While I had my knife out, I cut Shackleford's clothes off. We would take those and the comforter back with us and wash them in bleach before disposing of them.

Dragging the body was still awkward, but Lucas did not seem to be in as much distress. We were also moving faster, both of us able to watch where we were stepping now. The comforter slid fairly easily over the grass, mud, and leaves.

When I could no longer see the minivan, I told Lucas to stop. We flipped the body off the comforter in between some trees. I made sure to gather all the bindings and pieces of his clothing, then Lucas rolled everything together inside the comforter.

I opened the shopping bag and pulled out the five pounds of barbecued brisket I had bought. I dumped the contents of the container all over the body. The odor of barbecue sauce filled the air.

Lucas made an inarticulate noise. I turned to see him retching into the nearest shrub.

Perhaps I should have asked him if he wanted to leave before I poured the brisket onto the body.

The sound of something moving among the trees nearby spurred me to shove the brisket container into its bag, grab the rolled-up comforter, and haul a still-vomiting Lucas by the arm toward the minivan.

CHAPTER 6
LUCAS

WHEN I'D AGREED—*HAD* I AGREED?—TO HELP Phillip dispose of Alan Shackleford's body, the act had been an abstract concept. I'd somehow handled wrapping the body in the comforter and holding the horrifyingly inflexible legs as I carried it down the stairs. I'd been creeped out, sure, but all of that needed to be done so I did it.

I guess I'd imagined we'd just drop the body in the woods and leave. Even when Phillip had mentioned the feral hogs, their consuming the body wasn't something I thought about too hard.

But on the way to the woods, Phillip had cut the clothes off the body.

I'd never met Alan Shackleford when he was alive, and I was grateful for that. Not only would I have had to commit several illegal acts of violence on him for his abuse of my nephews, but I wouldn't have had Phillip to help me afterward.

But seeing Shackleford's naked body in the light of my headlamp, stiff in its curled-up position, drove home that this had been a person. Evil he might have been, and he deserved to be dead, but my sister had had a relationship with this guy.

My stomach had expressed its discomfort.

But I'd breathed through the nausea, and I thought things would be fine. We were almost to the woods, where we'd just leave the body then turn around and go home.

But the body had made a *thud* as we'd tipped it off the comforter and onto the grass and dirt. I did not need that sound in my memories.

And then—*and then*—fucking Phillip had pulled out a tub of barbecued meat and dumped it out all over the body. Just casually, like he did it all the fucking time.

It had made *splat* sounds as it hit Shackleford's dead flesh.

And that's when my brain connected the dots. We weren't just leaving the body here to slowly decompose in the chilly and humid Texas air. No, we were leaving the body here to be *eaten* by animals.

And that's when I threw up the coffee I'd just drunk. At least I hadn't had any dinner.

I was still mid-spasm when Phillip grabbed my arm and yanked me upright.

"Come on," he said. "The feral hogs are here."

Oh, shit.

I did my best to control my retching, and I was mostly able to walk on my own by the time we emerged from the trees. Phillip relaxed and released my arm.

I spat one more time and ran my sleeve over my mouth. "Sorry," I said.

The light from Phillip's headlamp moved from side to side as he shook his head. "It's my fault. I forgot not everyone is experienced in this sort of task."

We were about twenty feet from the minivan when Phillip put an arm across my chest, stopping me. He dropped the comforter and his shopping bag with the—*gag*—brisket container in it. Then instantly he produced a gun from somewhere and was pointing it toward the minivan. He'd been armed this whole time? Then I could've slapped myself. Of course he'd been armed. We were dumping a body in the middle of the woods with dangerous animals, and he was some sort of ex-spy or mafia guy or something.

Phillip whispered, "Take out your flashlight and point it at the rear wheel."

My self-preservation instincts finally kicked in. Phillip had pulled his gun out for a reason.

The little flashlight didn't look very powerful, but combined with our headlamps it lit up the area like a rock concert.

"*Aww*!" I tilted the flashlight a little to the side so I didn't blind the dog and her puppies.

Leaving Phillip and his gun behind, I approached the dogs at an angle, keeping my side toward them instead of coming at them straight on. One thing about growing up in an abusive household, you learned how to interact with other victims.

The dog was maybe 30 pounds, with short hair like a lab. Mostly tan with some white on her chest, belly, and legs. Her ears stood up like a deer's. She watched me nervously, keeping herself between me and her puppies. I couldn't see much of them, just two tiny brown furballs hunkered down in the icy cold grass.

"Hi, beautiful," I said in my most relaxed voice. I kept the same tone. "Hey, Phillip, do you have any food in your backpack, or is it all in the car?"

The dog switched her attention briefly to the woods, and I was very glad my ears were not as keen as hers.

"I have water bottles in the backpack but no food," he said.

I grimaced. I'd love to have one of those water bottles to rinse my mouth out. But that could wait.

"Can you pour some of the water in the—*hrrgh*—brisket container?"

"I will."

I got my gag reflex back under control. "Okay, gorgeous," I said to the dog. "Phillip's going to get you some water that'll taste like barbecue sauce. It's not food but it's the closest thing we have. I'll do my best not to vomit when I smell it, but can I tell you it'll be a cold day in hell before I ever eat barbecue again?"

I was within about five feet of the dog, who had backed up against the wheel of the minivan. At least she wouldn't run and leave her puppies, but I didn't want to put her in a position of feeling like she needed to snap at us to keep us away.

I turned my headlamp so it pointed to the side, and I shut off the flashlight. "I'm going to sit down right here in the grass and mud, and Phillip's going to bring the bowl of water over to me. Very very slowly."

I sat down, which on one hand was a relief because I was absolutely exhausted. But on the other hand, the ground was freezing, and my Tom Ford pants would never be the same.

I heard the rustle of the plastic shopping bag, then the crack of the water bottle being opened. Phillip poured the water into the container, and the dog twitched her ears and sniffed.

"Yeah, I bet that smells good to you. Not to me, but this is about you. You can have some food after we get you in the car. What a good dog you are, caring for your puppies." She'd probably come to the minivan because humans were a safer bet than the feral hogs.

Phillip walked over in an unhurried manner and handed me the container of water. It was murky with barbecue sauce, and even breathing through my mouth didn't keep the sweet-spicy smell at bay.

Phillip dropped something on the ground next to me before backing away. I ignored whatever it was for now and held my breath—more to stop smelling the barbecue sauce than out of any dramatic tension—as I slowly put the water down as close to the dog as I could reach.

The dog licked her lips, her eyes darting between me and the water.

"Go on," I crooned. "It's okay."

I put my left hand down at my side and felt a coiled rope. As I ran my fingers over it, I discovered a loop in one end like a lasso. Perfect, as long as I could get close enough to the dog.

She took a step toward the water, the whites of her eyes showing. Bit by bit she shifted herself in the direction of the bowl. I kept talking to her so she'd get used to my voice.

Finally she put her head down and lapped at the water, her eyes on me the entire time. I continued to talk nonsense.

When she lifted her head from the bowl, I carefully leaned forward and put my hand palm-up on the ground between us.

The dog glanced back at the puppies then gave me another good once-over.

"That's right. The puppies are fine. They'll be even better if we can get them out of the cold. You too, of course. I guess you're coming back with me and Phillip. I hope he's okay with that."

The dog walked over and sniffed my hand. I curled my fingers and brushed them under her chin. She leaned into my touch, and soon I was able to run my hand down her neck and scratch her chest.

How to get the rope over her head? I didn't want to scare her. Dawn was coming and Phillip and I needed to be on the road.

The dog made the question moot by crawling into my lap. I heard Phillip snort a laugh behind me.

Quickly I put an arm around her and pulled her into the warmth of my chest. I held the rope in my left hand and ran it up her shoulder and over her head. She didn't react when I tightened the loop around her neck.

"Okay, Phillip, I've got her." I nudged her off my lap. "Let's go get your puppies, huh?"

She stayed close by my leg as I led her over to the puppies, who were shivering violently.

"Holy crap, they're so small!" I exclaimed.

Phillip came up behind me. He'd turned his headlamp off, and he was holding the comforter we'd used to transport the body.

I made a face, but we didn't have anything else except Robin and Seth's Christmas gifts, and I'd rather keep those clean.

Phillip held his hand out to the dog, and she sniffed, giving him a slight tail wag. She watched him put the comforter on the ground and move the puppies onto it, but she didn't seem concerned.

I cleared my throat. "Um, I should have asked. Are you okay having the dogs in the house?"

He nodded. "That will be fine. I like dogs." He lifted the comforter and gave me a wry smile. "You do understand you have just adopted all three of them, right?"

I gave him a grin. "Three dogs to go with the three humans I adopted tonight."

I pretended not to notice the way his head jerked around toward me. Hah, if he thought he was going to vanish from the boys' lives—from *our* lives—after everything he'd done for us, he was sorely mistaken.

We got the dog and puppies settled into the back seat. Phillip gave the mother dog a sausage from inside one of the breakfast pastries along with a couple of pieces of cheese.

I was handed a bottle of water, but I declined any food.

"Looks like we're stopping at Buc-ee's again for dog food," I sighed. "Fucking hell, that entire place smells like barbecue sauce."

Phillip smirked. "I can go in alone. You stay in the car with the dogs."

The sun was just peeking over the horizon as we got back on the highway.

I yawned, but I was determined to stay awake on the trip home.

Phillip said, "Here." He handed me his phone. "I gave Robin a burner phone with my number in it, but I did not have yours. You could text him and tell him we will be back in a couple of hours."

I copied Robin's number into my phone. I sent the text, barely restraining myself from adding a photo of the puppies. It would be more fun for the dogs to be a surprise.

The three dogs were fast asleep on the comforter in the back seat. They probably needed baths. They definitely needed a visit to the vet.

"I wonder if Cole Washburn knows a vet who'd be open today. I don't imagine many of them have Christmas day hours," I said.

"He probably does," Phillip said. "But tomorrow's Monday and I do not think it will hurt anything to wait a day to get them checked out." Then he added. "But I will see if Buc-ee's has some dewormer and flea control medication at least."

"Wait a minute," I said, turning in my seat to stare at Phillip. His face in the morning sun was beautiful. I blinked. "Um, yeah. So how do you know Cole anyway?"

He smiled. "My next-door neighbor in the apartment complex, Steve, is one of Cole's business partners in a dating app they are developing."

I remembered reading about that. "Right. It's for people who get sidelined on traditional dating apps, right?"

Phillip nodded. "Yes. When Seth wrote that letter to Santa and asked for the message to be passed to you, Steve contacted Cole."

"Got it. I'm grateful it worked out the way it did."

Phillip winced. "It almost did not. I told my students I would not read their letters." He paused. "It is a long story I can tell you another time, but Steve and his boyfriend Baz read them."

He exited the highway. Buc-ee's looked even bigger in the sunlight.

"Would you mind getting me a coffee?" I asked Phillip.

He raised one eyebrow. "You mean one part coffee, twelve parts sugar?"

I smiled. "I'm impressed you remembered."

Shaking his head, Phillip pulled up next to a gas pump. He said, "I will go inside and pay cash for $30 worth of gas. The pump will turn on once I have paid."

"Okay, thanks."

He nodded and handed me the keys. His fingers were long, and I almost startled myself by imagining them wrapped around my dick.

I stifled a disbelieving chuckle. My dick hadn't stirred in ages, and it wanted this guy who used to work for the mob or something? But damn if he wasn't sexy. And strong. And protective.

Oblivious to my thoughts, Phillip exited the car and strode across the parking lot. His ass looked fantastic in those pants.

Right. I was supposed to be getting gas.

Once the pump activated, I started filling the tank. The minivan was looking the worse for wear, covered in mud and leaves, so I stopped pumping gas with $10 left and when the screen asked me if I wanted to add a car wash, I pressed *Yes*.

Phillip came back, a coffee tray in one hand and two large shopping bags in the other.

After handing me the coffee he opened one of the shopping bags and pulled out a throw blanket—with a cartoon beaver on it, of course.

He asked, "Will you help me put this under the dogs? I do not want the boys to have to see that comforter again."

I said, "Sure." But inside my heart was telling me what a thoughtful, wonderful man Phillip was.

Oh. *Oh.*

I didn't just find Phillip sexually attractive. Apparently romance was also on the table. Great. I was pretty sure mobbed-up guys weren't allowed to have boyfriends. And he'd probably rather have a girlfriend anyway.

Instead of just sliding the comforter out from under the dogs, I put the mother dog's new collar—pink with cartoon beavers—on her and led her out of the car for a quick walk to the nearest grass patch on her new leash—brown leather with a beaver embossed on a metal tag.

I couldn't wait until Phillip saw the presents I'd bought for all of us when we'd been here earlier.

When the dog and I returned to the minivan, Phillip had laid the throw blanket across the back seat. The puppies were moving around restlessly, searching for their mother. He'd put little Christmas bows around their necks.

The mother dog hopped up and laid down so the puppies could nurse. I stroked her head. "Good dog," I told her.

I helped Phillip roll up the comforter and put it in the rear cargo area. Then we both cleaned up with alcohol wipes. I couldn't wait to get a shower.

Phillip made as if to get in the driver's seat again, but I put my hand out. "Let me drive. It's your turn to nap."

He searched my face before nodding. "Fine, but I won't sleep. I am unable to sleep in the same space as someone else unless I really trust them." He gave a wry smile. "It might seem like an eternity, but we have only known each other for a few hours now."

What a lonely life he must have led. Interesting that he'd gone into teaching.

"I understand," I told him. "But maybe you can close your eyes at least."

We got in the car. Phillip nodded approvingly when we went through the drive-through car wash, which made me feel like I'd accomplished something meaningful.

I'd been worried the dog would freak out, but she and the puppies slept through the whole thing.

Phillip dug in one of the bags and handed me a breakfast taco.

"I refrained from choosing the brisket one for either of us," he said.

"You have my eternal gratitude," I told him as I unwrapped my bacon, egg, and cheese taco. My appetite was back with a vengeance.

I finished two tacos by the time we exited the car wash. Phillip pressed another bottle of water on me.

"You need to hydrate. Your body is still healing, and the coffee is not enough."

I felt like I should snark at him for managing me, but to be honest his concern made me feel warm and gooey inside. So I just said, "Thanks," and drank the water.

As we merged onto the highway, I turned the radio on low, and told Phillip, "Why don't you lean your seat back and chill? I know you won't sleep, but closing your eyes might help a little anyway."

"Sure. Good idea." He pressed the button to tilt back his seat, then he crossed his arms and went still.

Not five minutes later Phillip was breathing with a slight snore. I grinned, feeling pleased and proud of myself that I'd already earned the trust of the big bad mob enforcer, or secret agent, or whatever he'd been in his previous life.

I kept glancing over at Phillip. He was a beautiful man, which of course I'd noticed before. But he was kind too. Maybe he was into men. I could hope at least.

Phillip woke about thirty minutes later when his phone's text notification chimed. He sat up in a rush, his hands raised defensively in front of him.

I glanced over. "You okay, Phillip?"

He ran a hand over his face. "Uh, I... yes. I did not mean to sleep."

I grinned. "No worries. I'm sure you needed it. Can you see if that text was Robin?"

He rubbed his eyes again and took a sip from his water bottle before picking up his phone. "It is Robin. They found some containers of holiday decorations in the garage, and they would like to put them up."

He typed and sent a message. "I told them that was fine."

I sighed. "I wish they'd get some sleep, but they've had a pretty traumatic night."

"I believe they will sleep when we do this afternoon. After we get the dogs bathed and give the boys their presents, we should take them for brunch somewhere. They will not have any trouble sleeping once their bellies are full and the excitement has worn off."

I said, "The puppies should distract them enough that they won't notice us bringing in the bags of gifts, don't you think?"

Phillip nodded. "You help the boys with the dog baths, and I will unload the car."

"Okay," I said, "but you're not allowed to open my bags. I don't want to spoil the surprise."

Phillip eyed me suspiciously, but he agreed.

CHAPTER 7
PHILLIP

Was this hell?

Had karma caught up to me and decided *this* was the way to extract payback for all the morally gray acts I had committed during my lifetime?

I rubbed the cheap fabric between my fingers and looked resignedly into Seth's hopeful expression.

"Fine."

I stood up to cheers from not only Seth but also Robin and a smirking Lucas, the instigator of this particular torture.

Up until now, the morning had been pleasant.

The boys were ecstatic about the dogs, and giving them baths had been an excellent distraction. I had brought the shopping bags inside without them noticing. I had also retrieved the comforter from the minivan and put it in the wash without the boys being the wiser.

Robin and Seth had indeed decorated the house. A wreath adorned the front door, and an artificial tree festooned with red and gold balls stood in the corner of the living room. The fireplace mantel sported a garland of artificial greenery and red and gold bows.

Lucas and I complimented the boys on their efforts. After Seth and Robin had gotten the mother dog, now named Holly, settled in her new bed with the puppies, named Buddy and Peppermint, Lucas distributed the paltry presents we had procured for them.

“I’m sorry nothing is wrapped,” Lucas said.

Robin pressed his lips together, stroking the fleece jacket I had bought for him. “Seth and I didn’t expect to even have a Christmas this year. This is....” He turned his head and wiped his eyes.

Lucas went over and knelt beside Robin’s chair to give him a hug. I nodded to myself. Once again he had cemented the rightness of his position as the boys’ guardian. I would be able to leave them in his hands without worry.

And maybe I would still see Seth regularly at school, at least until Lucas moved the boys to wherever he decided to relocate to. He would need a house with a big yard. I had never really thought about George and Kathy’s back yard before, but Lucas could do worse than to choose a home with something like the large deck, big grassy area, and fenced-off pool this house boasted.

As I was lost in thought about Lucas, Seth, and Robin’s housing needs, Lucas pulled out the items he had not allowed me to watch him purchase at Buc-ee’s.

Onesies.

Beaver onesies.

Four of them.

Not three. *Four*.

One of which was in my size.

My death stare had not intimidated Lucas in the least, and I had just discovered I was susceptible to Seth's pleading eyes when he asked for a Christmas morning photo of all of us in our matching outfits.

The onesie was not large enough to go on over our clothing, so I followed Lucas into the primary bedroom to change.

"I found some restaurants that are open for brunch today," I told Lucas as I efficiently stripped down to my dark blue silk boxers.

"Uh," he responded faintly. His eyes scanned my body, and he swallowed. Then he blinked, and his eyes jerked up to meet mine.

I raised an eyebrow, and his cheeks flushed. He said, "Sorry. Um, I'm gay, in case you didn't know. I mean, it's public information, but not everyone reads the tabloids."

I shrugged. "It is a natural reaction. And I knew." I had researched Lucas after all.

"You, ah, don't have a problem with it?" His eyes slid down to where his hands were fiddling with the hem of his shirt.

"With your being gay? No."

He looked up again. "Uh, I mean, I'm assuming you're straight?"

Oh.

I could have smacked myself.

"I am pan but I am demisexual. And I am sorry but I have not slept in over twenty-four hours, so if you have been flirting with me I missed it." On jobs I kept an eye out for flirting from targets, but when I was off-duty I rarely thought about it.

Lucas' face turned even more red. "Um, I wanted to? But I was worried you were straight, and you can obviously kick my ass, so I was kind of holding off...." He turned away and whipped his sweater over his head. His ribs were too prominent, and his skin did not have a healthy color.

I stepped into the onesie, buying myself time to come up with a response.

I went with, "I do not want to give you the impression I am brushing you off. I am flattered, but I need to know someone better before I become interested in them sexually."

I zipped up the onesie and met his gaze. His eyes flicked over me before he looked away. I saw his lips quirk upward before he rubbed his mouth.

I scowled. "And forcing me to dress in this ridiculous costume is not enhancing your charm."

He laughed then. "Sorry," he gasped. "It's just...." He flapped his hand in my direction, then covered his mouth again and pretended to cough. "Ahem. Uh, right. Yes."

He positioned himself to face away from me and pulled off his pants. He was too thin from his alcohol abuse and his withdrawal, but he would regain the weight with a few weeks of healthy eating.

He shook out his onesie, preparing to step into it. "Thank you for telling me about your being demi. Um." He darted a glance at me. "Would it be too pushy of me to check in with you periodically about whether you'd be open to going on a date?"

I put my hands on my hips, pleased but slightly exasperated. "I am demisexual, not demiromantic. I am open to going on a date *now*, as long as you are not expecting me to sleep with you."

Lucas froze, his hand ready to zip up his onesie. Unfortunately the zipper pull was level with his crotch, which gave him the distracting pose of someone cupping their genitals.

"Oh," he said, his eyes widening. "*Oh*. I see. I get the difference. Right." Then a big smile bloomed across his face. "Right! Yes. Um, will you go on a date with me? Maybe this week sometime? No sex involved, I promise."

"Fine."

At last he pulled up his zipper, giving me a frown. "*Fine*? That's not a lot of enthusiasm there, Phillip."

I raised one eyebrow at him. "You have not earned my enthusiasm yet, Lucas." I strode toward the door in my onesie, my head held high.

Seth was coming toward the bedroom, probably to find out why Lucas and I were taking so long. He grinned in delight when he saw me. "Uncle Phillip! You're wearing it!" He spun around and raced back to the living room, the tail of his onesie dragging along the floor as he shouted for Robin to come see.

I stopped in the middle of the hall, frozen. Lucas came up behind me and put a reassuring hand on my back.

I blinked at him, wide-eyed, still trying to process this development.

Lucas smiled. "Welcome to the family, *Uncle* Phillip." Then he tugged on my tail, flipped the hood of the onesie over my head, and pushed me forward. "Come on, it's family portrait time!"

An hour later, seated on the outdoor patio of a restaurant, I could not stop looking at the photo Lucas had texted to my phone. I had glanced at it after it had been taken, but I had not had time to consider it in detail until now.

Everyone had ordered and we were waiting for our food. None of us had showered, though Lucas had put on clean clothes at least. Not having that option, I had merely put my suit pants on with my black t-shirt and black jacket. And the gun in my ankle holster of course.

The day was pleasant, the heaters on the restaurant's patio chasing away any chill in the air. I was between Lucas and Seth, with Robin across the round table from me.

"Can we get the picture framed?" Seth asked Lucas. He did not mean the numerous photos of the dogs the boys had taken. No, he meant what Lucas had called the *family portrait.*

And I could not deny that was exactly what it looked like. The four of us were in our beaver onesies. Seth, Lucas, me, and Robin all in a row. Lucas, with his arms around me and Seth, sported a grin identical to the boys', making it obvious they were related. I, however, was not exactly smiling.

One of my arms was around Lucas' waist, and my other hand was on Robin's shoulder, pulling him into me. Possessive. That was what my expression was. As if now that I had been invited to be a part of this family, I would defend them to the death.

Which was not an exaggeration, though I had already been prepared to do exactly that even before Seth had called me *Uncle Phillip*.

I pulled up my text messages and opened my thread with Ripley.

Merry Christmas. I have been adopted.

[Photo]

My phone chimed almost immediately, but it was not Ripley. It was Steve, my next-door neighbor at the apartment.

STEVE

Just making sure you're okay. Also, Merry Christmas!

[Photo]

After a moment, Steve replied.

STEVE

Holy horse hockey, Phillip! Twelve hours ago you were a mild-mannered substitute teacher with a violent origin story, and now you've formed a beaver cult with a hot TV actor and his nephews?

I have skills you could only dream of.

And then Ripley finally replied.

RIPLEY

I... have no words. Except you look proud to be a beaver or whatever the fuck those things are supposed to be.

Lucky I finished bulletproofing your alias last night

I frowned.

I thought it HAD been bulletproofed.

RIPLEY

Sure, against nosy school districts and FBI background checks. Now it can withstand TMZ.

[GIF of Blanche from The Golden Girls saying "Damn, I'm good."]

"Is everything okay?" Lucas put his hand on my leg, just above my knee.

I shut off my phone. "Sorry," I said. "Ripley—my computer-savvy friend I told you about—and my neighbor Steve were wishing me a Merry Christmas."

Lucas smiled, but it seemed strained.

"Are you okay?" I asked him quietly. He had just gotten out of rehab yesterday after all.

He gave me a half-shrug.

I leaned closer so our shoulders were touching. Lucas' entire forearm rested on my thigh, his hand on my knee. I told him, "You can talk to me, you know. I won't share your private information."

He sighed, glancing across the table to where the boys were chatting. "I don't have those," he said. "Friends, I mean. None that would just text me for no reason." He rubbed his thumb through the condensation on his orange juice glass. "I used to." His mouth twisted. "Before the drugs and the booze.

After that I only had friends I partied with. No one else wanted to be around me."

"With good reason," I observed. I laid my hand across the back of his.

"Yeah." He ducked his head a little.

"But there is time to make new friends."

"I hope so."

Our food arrived then, and I missed the feel of Lucas' body next to mine, his hand on my knee. I found myself oddly concerned about what day we would go on our date, and if I would have to remind Lucas about it to confirm we were actually going.

I was tired, I reminded myself. My body was overdue for some real sleep, not the light doze I had had in the car. Though that had been nothing short of astonishing. I could not remember the last time I had slept in the same room with another person, much less a person I did not know well.

Sleep would be first on the agenda when we returned to the house.

I would deal with staging Alan Shackleford's disappearance after night fell.

And at some point I should stop by my apartment and pick up some clothes.

While all these thoughts were vying for my attention, I monitored everyone's food consumption. Seth and Robin were eating well, but Lucas was picking at his French toast.

I nudged him. "Are you not hungry?"

He shrugged. "Not really. I ate those breakfast tacos earlier. But my appetite's been off since rehab."

I nodded, mentally cataloging what I had seen of the contents of George and Katrina's kitchen cabinets. They must have a blender somewhere. I would get Lucas some protein powder and ingredients to make smoothies. I said, "Understandable. Do you want to bring that back to the house?"

He shook his head. "I won't eat it."

"Okay. We can order some groceries to be delivered this afternoon. Maybe you will feel more like eating then."

"Uncle Phillip, I'm tired," Seth said from my other side. He leaned across the gap between our chairs and put his head on my chest. My arm automatically came up around him and I found myself pressing a kiss to the top of his head.

Refusing to analyze that action, I told him, "We will all go back to the house and take some long naps."

"Mmmm-kay." He went limp against me.

Across the table, Robin raised his eyebrows at his brother but gave me a small smile.

I looked over at Lucas, and I was stunned by the expression on his face. Surely I was misreading that look, but it certainly seemed to be the same type of possessiveness I had been feeling when the photo had been taken earlier.

That I was feeling now.

Lucas put his hand on the back of my chair.

My arm tightened around Seth, and I nodded at Lucas.

We had things to discuss after our naps.

CHAPTER 8
LUCAS

I'd expected to have to argue with Phillip to get him to nap with me in the primary bedroom. I'd had my justifications lined up, ready to be used to make my case.

But instead he'd just said, "Okay."

Then he'd stripped down to those silk boxers that clung to his body, hiding nothing. Holy fuck, that ass. And his back. I licked my lips, staring as he slid between the sheets.

He pulled a pillow under his head and settled into a slightly curled position on his side facing me where I stood in the middle of the room. After a moment he opened his eyes and glared. "Are you going to sleep or just stand there?"

I couldn't stop my lips from turning up. "Sorry. Just admiring the view." Then I froze. "Uh, is that okay? I'm not trying to push you into sex or anything."

His brow furrowed then cleared. "Flirting is fine, Lucas. I should have clarified that earlier. I do not mind being touched either, if is not sexual."

I let out a breath and nodded. “Thanks, that helps.” I’d meant what I’d told Phillip about not pressuring him for sex until he was ready. Hell, my body was iffy enough about the idea I didn’t mind waiting.

But I could still give him an idea of what he’d be getting when the time came, right?

Because if that man could show off his abs and his fucking back muscles—how had I never appreciated back muscles before?—not to mention his bubble butt and the outline of his sizeable dick, well, I could show off my unhealthy pallor, my concave stomach, and my overall lack of muscle tone.

Shit.

I dropped my head to my chest and tossed my jeans onto the chair in the corner of the room.

“Come to bed, Lucas. I do not know what you are thinking about over there, but it cannot be worth staying awake for.”

Wasn’t that the fucking truth?

Deciding to worry about my lack of physical appeal later, I got into bed and positioned myself several respectful inches away from Phillip.

“Lucas,” he said grumpily.

“What?” I snapped.

He lifted his head off the pillow. “I am impressed I was able to nap in the car with you, but I guarantee I will not be able to sleep now if you do not relax.” He hesitated. “Can I…?” He gestured between us.

I frowned. “Get closer you mean? Sure.”

He huffed, then reached out and slung his arm over my chest. He dragged me across the gap between us and I found myself on my side being spooned. Phillip tucked a pillow under my head, making sure my neck was supported. Then he draped his arm over my waist and laid his hand against my chest.

Okay. Not what I was expecting.

Though I hadn't expected any of the past twenty-four hours. I doubted the therapists at rehab would've recommended I take responsibility for my nephews, help dispose of a dead body, and adopt some dogs. Oh, and sort of get a maybe-boyfriend. Who I hadn't kissed yet.

"Stop thinking," Phillip muttered.

It would be a miracle if I could sleep.

Phillip lifted his hand from my chest and put it on my forehead. "Relax these muscles."

"What?" I started to turn, but he pincered my forehead between his thumb and his forefinger. "Ow."

"Stay still. I will help you relax your facial muscles. You cannot sleep if your face is tense."

I scowled under his fingers. "My face isn't tense."

I felt his chest move up and down as he chuckled.

"Fuck you."

"Give me two minutes. If you are not relaxed by then, you can do whatever you want."

"Fine," I huffed.

I flopped my head back onto the pillow and shut my eyes.

Phillip took two fingers and swept them across my brow in a slow rhythm. That was kind of nice.

I concentrated on my facial muscles. Huh, maybe some of them were tense after all.

Phillip's fingers swept down onto my cheekbones.

When was the last time I'd slept with someone? Like to actually sleep? Probably my last relationship, which had been, shit, three years ago, maybe?

Well, I wouldn't be able to sleep now.

Phillip's fingers found my temples, and I was out.

I grunted in protest when Phillip, who had been deliciously wrapped around me, pulled his arms and body away before sitting up.

"Wha's matter?" I mumbled, trying to scooch under the covers.

"Both of our phones have been going off."

The bed only shifted slightly as he got up. Memory foam mattresses were wonderful. I smiled and snuggled down into my cocoon. The sheets were still warm from Phillip's body heat.

The mattress barely dipped when Phillip sat down again. I made a humming purr. "Get un' covers."

"Lucas, you need to wake up." Phillip's voice had the same note of stress in it he'd had when he was trying to get me away from the feral hogs.

I opened my eyes and, without moving out of my comfortable nest, whipped the sheet off my face. "What's wrong?" I wiped my mouth—drool, lovely—and blinked at him. He had both our phones in his hands.

"Look." He handed me his phone, browser opened to TMZ's home page.

My stomach dropped.

The second story down was headlined, "Lucas McCord Leaves Rehab for Christmas Date with Mystery Man and Kids in Texas". There was a photo of us from brunch. Robin's back was to the camera. Seth's face had been blurred out, but he was clearly leaning trustingly against Phillip's chest while Phillip had his arm around him. I had my hand on the back of Phillip's chair, and he and I were staring at each other like... like we were looking at our hearts' desires.

"Holy shit." It was all I could say. I knew I needed to strategize the potential publicity problems, but my brain didn't want to stop staring at the photo.

Finally I tore my eyes away from Phillip's phone and looked up at him. "I'm so sorry. I didn't see anyone with a camera. Is this going to be an issue for you, having your picture everywhere?"

He shook his head. "Not from the perspective of my former occupation, if that is what you are worried about. The people who knew me then are either dead or friendly. I made sure of it."

"Uh, okay." I decided I didn't want to know what that last sentence meant.

My phone beeped, and I reluctantly sat up as Phillip handed it to me. My agent had texted.

FELICIA

Call me right the fuck now!

I looked at my other texts and I had a similar message from Bridgette, my publicist.

"Phillip," I started. But what could I say?

"Do it," he said.

"Huh?" I looked up to see an expression on his face that seemed to be a combination of amused and impatient.

"Tell them we are together. Tell them I am your nephew's teacher and that is how we met." He shrugged. "We can say we were keeping it quiet until my substitute teaching term ends in January."

I furrowed my brow. "Why would you do that? You've got to be aware of what you'll have to deal with—the paparazzi, the made-up stories. Why would you put yourself through that?"

He smiled at me. "Because there is no sense in delaying the inevitable. This morning I decided you were mine. You, Seth, and Robin." He shrugged again. "As long as you agree, we might as well act like it from the beginning."

My mouth fell open. "What?" I felt my heart start beating faster.

He put his hand out and smoothed the wrinkles in my forehead before cupping my face. "I have seen a lot of shit in my life, and I have met a lot of shitty people. I learned how to tell the good people from the shitty ones. And you, Lucas McCord, are a good person."

Phillip's phone chimed.

I shook my head. "No, I've done some really awful stuff."

He put his thumb over my lips. "So you make amends if you want to. But your behavior, particularly related to your addiction, is not *you*." He searched my eyes. "After I read Seth's letter about how Shackleford was treating them, I confronted him and demonstrated the consequences if he continued his abuse. But I knew that living with him was not sustainable for the boys. I had to wrap up another project I was dealing with, but I finished that yesterday. I was already making plans to insert myself into Seth and Robin's lives, even before I knew they needed help disposing of Shackleford."

"What, uh, what was your plan regarding me? If you saw Seth's letter, you knew I might show up. And I'm sure you knew my reputation. I'm not exactly parent material."

He leaned over and kissed me on the forehead. "Like I said, I was going to insert myself into their lives. Sort of a family friend role to start. I would have given you the benefit of the doubt until you proved you were unfit to be their guardian."

My phone's text notification went off again.

I leaned back so his hand fell away from my face. I crossed my arms and narrowed my eyes at him. "And what exactly would you have done to me if you decided I was unfit?"

He grinned. "Nothing like you might be imagining. I would have created a situation where you would have been incented to sign over your guardianship rights."

"Or you would have had them taken from me."

He shrugged again. "I am sure you agree Robin and Seth's well-being is more important than the pride of your imaginary unfit alter ego. Fortunately that will not be an issue. I have no doubts the real you is fit to be a parent."

I looked away, blowing out a breath. "I wish I was as confident as you. I'm scared shitless."

"Well, you will not have to do it alone if you do not wish to."

That brought my head around to face him again. I kind of didn't want to know the answer to my next question, but avoiding my problems had been a big reason for my drug and alcohol use, so I was going to ask it anyway.

"Are you pretending you want to be with me because it'll guarantee you can remain involved with the kids?"

I could feel myself turning red, and my heart was pounding, but I watched him closely to see what he'd say.

My phone beeped again.

Phillip tilted his head, then he reached out and pried one of my hands from where they were crossed over my chest.

"I did wonder what it would be like to take care of them myself in the event you did not come for them. But the prospect of parenting, particularly by myself, was daunting, as you acknowledged." He turned my hand over and stroked my palm. "But there you were. Sitting in that dingy hallway, obviously unwell and exhausted. You came as soon as you could, as soon as you found out about Seth and Robin. You were there for them, even though it appeared you did not have anyone who would be there for you."

He leaned in and pressed a chaste, soft kiss to my lips. "How could I resist you?"

CHAPTER 9
PHILLIP

Lucas' eyes welled with tears. "But why are you so sure? You know I'm a screw-up. I'm scared I'm going to ruin Robin and Seth's lives, and I'm afraid I'm going to do something to push you away." He gripped my hand tightly. "Not to mention, this is crazy. We haven't even known each other twenty-four hours. We've never kissed, not really, much less been on a date. How can you know we'll work out?"

My phone chimed twice in a row.

I put my arm around Lucas and tucked him against my side.

"I could be wrong, Lucas. I am not infallible. But I have had to rely on my gut in life-or-death situations over and over again. And my gut is telling me my future is with you." I took his chin in my free hand, loving the feel of his beard against my fingers. "I get that you need time. But," I gestured at our phones lying on the bed a few feet away. "I think you are going to have to decide sooner rather than later."

Lucas' phone beeped again.

He snorted. "You mean now." He pressed his face into my chest.

His phone beeped yet again.

Lucas made a face against my skin. "What if I relapse?"

I put my finger under his chin until he looked up at me. "What if you do not? I know it will not be easy, but you were strong enough to check yourself into rehab, and now you have even more motivation to stay sober than you did then. Do you have a sponsor or a therapist? Someone you can call if you get in a bad place mentally?"

"I've got a month of outpatient visits with the therapist at the rehab facility, so that will give me time to find a new one." He grimaced. "I don't like the twelve-step programs; they're mostly religion-based." He shuddered. "My father was a preacher. Church talk is more likely to make me want to drink than help me stop."

I nodded. "We may be able to find a non-religious support group as well, depending on where you end up choosing to live. There have to be LGBT-friendly ones."

His head jerked up sharply. "Where *I* choose to live.... Are you... are you set on staying here in Bent Oak?"

My phone chimed.

"I have a few more weeks of my substitute teaching commitment. But if you have a strong desire to live somewhere else, I could see about finding a replacement." I glanced around the room. "I will have to decide what to do with the house."

Lucas swallowed. "I don't have anywhere in particular I want to live. I'm more concerned about the boys. I need to talk to someone to see if they'd be better off staying here in Bent Oak or starting fresh in a completely different environment."

I squeezed Lucas' hands. "That is an important consideration. My other house is in northern California, but it is in a very remote location. I think we would be better off somewhere with more infrastructure for schools and mental health resources."

He smiled and his eyes were intent on mine. "We? Are you really sure?"

"I am. Are you?"

His phone beeped again.

"Fuck it, I am." He surged toward me and caught my mouth in a kiss. It started as a quick peck, but he came back again and the kiss turned sensual, our tongues meeting for the first time.

Lucas' phone rang and he broke away. "Fuck."

Sighing, he picked up his phone. He leaned against me and answered it. "Yes, Felicia, I saw the photo."

Smiling, I put one arm around Lucas and picked up my own phone with the other hand. I had never felt such a sense of anticipation about the future.

The beaver onesie family portrait broke the internet.

After the brunch photo went online, Lucas' agent and publicist had been over the moon about him having not only a romantic partner but also two heretofore unknown nephews to care for. They thought a family was exactly what he needed to convert his reputation from drunken partier to serious actor.

Lucas protested that he was not using his family to change his image, and he was smartly told to just enjoy the happy side effects of his new life.

"They want me to trot you and the boys around like I'm showing you off," he complained after hanging up the phone. Then he sighed. "But Felicia says the studio might consider me more strongly for a superhero role I auditioned for a couple of months ago now that I'm some sort of bastion of stability."

"Do you want the role?" I asked him.

He nodded. "But not at the expense of your privacy. And there's no way I'm exposing the boys to the tabloids if I can help it."

"Well, I agree about the boys, but I am willing to be shown off if it will help you get a role you want. Besides, you will need the payday from a big-budget film like that. Robin and Seth will want to go to college."

Lucas shook his head, but later he approved a short statement to be released to the press stating we were in a relationship but requesting no one take photos of the boys.

I kept Ripley apprised of the publicity. He graciously volunteered to blur out the boys' faces on our Christmas morning family portrait, and Lucas uploaded that version to his social media accounts.

Hours later the photo had spawned memes, most Buc-ee's locations were starting to sell out of their onesies, and Lucas and I had a relationship name.

Phicas.

Which was apparently pronounced "ficus".

Like the tree.

Ripley had celebrated this by adding a ficus tree to the background of the onesie portrait before hacking my phone and installing the doctored photo as my lockscreen image.

Steve had texted me a photo of a ficus tree and said, "Baz and I disavow any knowledge of what you're up to, but let us know if you want any help!"

Dirk Derry, one of Steve's brothers who was part of the band Melodious Moon, had texted as well.

DIRK

Dude, what happened to you? You're some family man now? You in that onesie gave me the best laugh I've had all year. But, seriously, are you okay? Text back "I'm fine" if you need rescuing

It was odd to consider that for the past several years my only friends had been Ripley, George, and Katrina. George and Katrina's deaths had cut that group down to just Ripley.

But now I had multiple people I would call my friends. And they knew about my background and had not run away screaming.

And there was Lucas. My chest felt warm thinking of his vulnerability when we had discussed our future earlier. He might not see why I wanted to be with him, but in reality I was amazed he was willing to be with me. Retired operatives were not on anyone's relationship wish list.

Robin and Seth had seemed pleased to learn Lucas and I were dating, though Robin gave us several side-eyed looks. I had been concerned that his mother and stepfather had fostered negative views of queer people in Robin, but he said he did not care about that. I made a mental note to pull him aside later and discuss any worries he might have.

Cole Washburn had texted Lucas to congratulate him on our relationship. He had invited us, along with Seth and Robin, to come to dinner after the new year out at the animal rescue ranch Cole ran with his two boyfriends.

By 7pm Lucas was visibly exhausted from the stress of dealing with everything. Our nap together seemed like it had been days ago instead of mere hours. We ordered pizza for dinner, and I was relieved when Lucas had eaten two slices. Afterward he slumped on the couch to watch a movie with Seth. The dogs curled up on the cushions next to them.

Robin was reading something on the burner phone. I really needed to get him a better one. And a computer. And a coat that did not have a beaver on it.

But all that would have to wait until tomorrow.

"Robin," I said. "Would you be willing to come with me to help me stage Shackleford's disappearance at the apartment?"

He did not have time to reply before Lucas said, "What?" He paused the movie. "No, I'll go with you. Robin doesn't need to go back to that apartment."

I held up a hand. "Lucas, even if you were in top physical shape, which you are not, I need Robin to help me go through the apartment one more time and make sure nothing important is left behind." Which was not completely true. Shackleford had been an idiot. If he had a hiding place in that apartment, it would not take more than a few minutes for me to find it. All I really needed Robin for was to pick me up after

I disposed of Shackleford's car. Lucas was in no condition to do that.

I tipped my head at Robin, who nodded and said, "I want to go. I'm so used to working all the time I'm not sure what to do with myself right now anyway."

Lucas, who had sat upright but had not stood up from the couch, asked Robin, "Are you sure you won't be bothered by being in that apartment again?"

Robin shook his head. "It'll be for the last time, and I want to do it."

I walked over to Lucas and bent down to kiss the corner of his mouth. "Rest. We will be back in a couple of hours." He relaxed back into the couch and nodded. I leaned over and kissed the top of Seth's head before turning to leave.

Seth said, "Um, are you going to be kissing us a lot?"

I paused and looked at him with a raised eyebrow. "I had intended to. You need to know I care about you. But now I realize I did not ask your consent. I am sorry. I should have gained your permission first. I appreciate your raising the issue."

He shrugged and looked down at one of the puppies. "Um, I mean, I don't mind. You can keep doing it. Mom used to, when I was real little. It's nice."

"Thank you for letting me know. If you change your mind at any time, you can ask me to stop and I will."

"Okay," he said, still looking down at the puppy. Seth and Robin's mother had died of a drug overdose. I was not surprised she had pulled away from her children over time. Frankly I had been shocked Alan Shackleford had avoided becoming addicted to drugs. But he had favored alcohol instead.

Robin was in the kitchen pulling on his new fleece jacket. He followed me into the garage, and I pressed the button to raise the door.

"Are we taking the minivan?" he asked.

"No. We're taking my SUV. It is registered under a completely different name." The SUV I drove to work at the elementary school was still parked at my apartment building. This one was from my former life.

I told Robin, "I need to get some stuff out of the back and put it in the garage before we leave. Do you want to drive?" I had ridden with Robin and Seth last night in Shackleford's ill-maintained muscle car on the way from the concert to their apartment. Robin had been a careful driver.

"For real?" I nodded and the biggest smile I had seen from him yet exploded across his face. "Yes, please!"

I smiled and handed him the key fob. "Pop the rear hatch." I showed him where the release was. I could have used the biometric lock on the hatch itself, but I wanted Robin to get familiar with the vehicle.

I took my second weapons bag from the secure compartment in the back of the SUV. It was too big to fit in the remaining space in George's gun safe, so I locked it in the trunk of the Maserati and pocketed the key.

After sending the garage door down, I jogged through the house and out the front door. Robin had my SUV running and had adjusted the seat and mirrors.

"Ready?" I climbed into the passenger seat.

He nodded and reversed out of the driveway. I could tell he was not expecting the power of the vehicle by the jerk when he accelerated down the street, but he quickly adapted. By the time we reached his former apartment building, he was driving confidently, a small smile on his face.

We ran into a couple of people on the stairs, but they did not give either of us a second look. I had checked for cameras on my first visit, and there were none.

The inside of the apartment was just as dreary as it had seemed the previous night. "It is a long shot," I told Robin, handing him a small flashlight and some nitrile gloves. "But can you check inside the vents in both bedrooms and in the bathroom? See if he was hiding anything in there."

Eyebrows raised, Robin put on the gloves then took the flashlight and headed toward the smaller bedroom. I went to the primary bedroom.

I gloved up as well. When I found a small suitcase in the closet, I unzipped it and put a reasonable amount of clothing and toiletries in it.

Then I searched. It turned out Shackleford was too lazy to unscrew the vents every time he wanted to access his secret stash of treasures. He had a cardboard box under the bed.

I handed Robin the stack of bills, probably about $800. "Do you have a bank account?" I asked him.

He shook his head. "My paychecks got direct deposited into Alan's account."

I closed my eyes and wished once again that I had killed Shackleford when I had had the chance.

"We will open accounts for you and for Seth tomorrow when we go get you your new phones and some clothes."

He said, "Will this be enough money for all that? I'm fine with the little phone you gave me last night, if that's okay?"

I finished transferring Seth and Robin's birth certificates and social security cards into the inside pocket of my jacket before facing Robin and putting my hands on his shoulders. I said, "Robin. I am sorry I was not being clear. That money is yours to keep. Hell, it probably came from your paychecks. Lucas and I will provide you and Seth allowances for spending money, but we will pay for all of your necessities. That includes a phone and clothing. Okay?"

Robin's eyes were round. "Um, okay."

I stuck the cardboard box back under the bed. "We need to get you a laptop as well. We should probably start a list."

"A laptop? Really?"

"You will need it for your GED and to apply to colleges when you are ready."

Robin looked thoughtful as he took the suitcase from me. "I don't know if I can get into college. My grades weren't great. I started working even before Mom died."

I did a cursory search of the living room and kitchen. "You can always start at community college, but you should apply everywhere anyway. Do you know what you would like to study?"

"Coding," he said without hesitation. "Software programming. I was doing pretty good with it before Mom died and Alan sold my laptop."

I nodded. "My friend Steve is the CEO of a company that is making a dating app. Perhaps he would have some recommendations about the best computer for you." Ripley, I was sure, would try to talk me into letting him make Robin a custom computer that would end up being powerful enough to run the New York Stock Exchange. Right now a store-bought laptop would be enough.

Robin went wide-eyed again. "I really don't need much. Just something, like you said, to go online and stuff. A computer for real software development would be too much."

I urged Robin out of the apartment. He carried the suitcase. Last night I had kept Shackleford's key ring, so I used that to lock up.

When we were on the stairs, I told Robin, "Your uncle has plenty of money. I have plenty of money. A more powerful laptop is a good investment in your future."

He frowned but nodded. When we got to the bottom of the stairs he said, "Do you think Uncle Lucas will start drinking again? Because I hated it when Alan drank. I like Uncle Lucas, but I don't think Seth should be around him if he's going to fall off the wagon."

I steered Robin toward Shackleford's car. "Addictions are powerful, and I cannot predict with 100% certainty whether Lucas will stay sober or not." I used Shackleford's key to open the trunk of the car. "But even though he has been in rehab before, this time he made the decision to go on his own. And now he has you and Seth, as well as me, to think about. I am very optimistic he will succeed, and I am going to make sure he has a therapist and a support network to help him." After Robin threw the suitcase in the trunk, I shut it. "But I promise you, if Lucas backslides and is no longer an ideal guardian for Seth, I will make sure either you or I are given custody of him."

Robin regarded me seriously for a long moment, then said, “Okay. I can live with that.”

“Good. Now I am going to take Shackleford’s car to a place where it will be—*hmmm*—taken care of. I will text you the address of a fast-food restaurant to drive my SUV to. Get yourself something to eat if you like, and I will meet you as soon as I can.”

“Got it.”

CHAPTER 10
PHILLIP

After I negotiated the delivery of Shackleford's car to a local chop shop, I found Robin polishing off the remains of a burger and fries. It had only been a couple of hours since he had inhaled four slices of pizza. I mentally berated myself for not realizing food would have been scarce for him and Seth.

I sat down across from him and stole one of his last French fries.

"Hey!"

I smirked and took one of his napkins as well to wipe my fingers off. "Do you need any more food? A milkshake?"

He looked longingly toward the counter where people were placing their orders, but shook his head. "No. I'd feel bad if I got one and Seth didn't."

My chest felt tight. "You are a good brother. After we go to my apartment, we can stop for something on the way back to the house."

Seeming relieved, Robin agreed. He quickly cleared the table of his trash, and then he was ready to go.

Robin drove us over to the apartment I had been living in since I had arrived in Bent Oak. I had prepaid a six-month lease just in case, but fortunately it had only taken a few weeks to avenge George and Katrina and to remove the threat to my third-grade students.

We got out of the elevator on the fourth floor. I pointed at my door and said, "This one is mine, but I would like to say hello to my neighbors first."

Robin shrugged. "Sure, whatever."

I felt my mouth turn up. "Do you like rabbits?"

"Uh... I guess?"

"Well, we are about to find out for certain."

I walked past my door to the next one on the same side of the hall and knocked. "Steve and Baz live here," I told Robin. "But they might be across the hall."

The door opened, and Baz's handsome face broke into a huge grin. "Well, well, well. If it isn't the darling of the tabloids." He turned his head around and shouted, "Steve, look who's here!" Then he opened the door wider and said, "Come on in!" He held out his hand to Robin. "Hey, I'm Baz." They shook hands and Robin introduced himself.

Steve, whose blond hair and striking blue eyes contrasted with Baz's more muted coloring of brown hair and brown eyes, came out of the kitchen carrying a large cardboard box with the top open. "Hey, Phillip! Oh, you must be Robin. I'm Steve. Welcome." He put the box down on the coffee table. "Come look. Their eyes are starting to open."

I hurried over to gaze into the box. "They are much bigger now."

The box was full of eight baby rabbits, each about the size of a person's fist. Their fur had grown in nicely, and Steve was right, some of them had their eyes open.

"Can I touch them?" Robin asked.

Steve said, "Sure, just use a couple of fingers."

Robin reached out and stroked two fingers down the back of the closest kit.

"They were born a week ago," I told him.

Baz, who had gone across the hall, came back into the apartment. "Dirk and Drake are going to come say hi. Those are Steve's younger brothers," he told Robin. He gestured at the box of baby rabbits. "They wanted some time to work on their music, so we were bunny-sitting."

"I stopped by to pick up some clothes," I told Baz and Steve.

I was certain they were about to start questioning me, but Dirk walked in, carrying Rocket, the mother rabbit. Drake was right behind him. The two were twins, and they were blond and blue-eyed just like Steve.

"Phillip!" Dirk shouted. "What's up with the family man lifestyle? You working undercover or something?"

Drake hissed at him and slapped the back of Dirk's head. Dirk put his hands up defensively and said, "What?"

Drake turned to Robin, "Please ignore my jerk of a brother. I'm Drake Derry, and this is Dirk."

Dirk grimaced in my direction, then said to Robin, "Shit, dude, sorry. I didn't see you there."

Robin tucked his shaggy hair behind his ear and, after blinking a few times, said hesitantly, "Uh, nice to meet you. My little brother and I were at your concert last night. And, no worries about what you said." He turned to me. "Those were good questions, and I guess that's been bothering me as well, ever since you and Uncle Lucas announced you were dating."

I regarded him calmly. "You want to know if we are pretending to date each other?" Why had I not discussed this with Robin before now?

Everyone in the room went still.

Robin's chin went up, and he said, "More like, are *you* pretending? I don't want you to think I don't appreciate what you've done for me and Seth, but Uncle Lucas is just out of rehab, and it seems a little fast for you to suddenly be his boyfriend."

"Your concern is understandable," I told him.

Steve said, "Uh, you want us to leave?"

I shook my head. "You are my friends, and I would tell you anyway. If Robin is agreeable, I would like you to know what is happening."

Robin shrugged and said, "Fine with me."

Dirk came over and held the rabbit out to Robin. "This is Rocket. You wanna hold her? She's good for helping me through big conversations."

Robin smiled and said, "Sure." He carefully put his hands around Rocket and took her from Dirk. Rocket sniffed him and then settled down in his arms and relaxed.

I said to Robin, "I am not pretending. Being attracted to your uncle and creating this almost instant family was not how I expected this weekend to turn out. But I am extremely happy it happened this way." I met his gaze. "I agree this is very soon to be announcing a relationship. In a world where you and Seth were not a consideration, Lucas and I would probably have just dated casually to see where things led."

I took a breath. "But you and Seth *are* a consideration, and even if our picture was not making the rounds of the internet, the two of you need stability, not uncertainty. So Lucas and I had a serious conversation about our attraction to each other, and we decided to date exclusively. I cannot promise this will last forever, but I would like it to.

Robin's forehead creased. "That's... I mean, you've known each other for less than twenty-four hours."

Steve said, "Well, sometimes you just know." I wondered if he had ever told his brothers that he and Baz had not even been on one date before they had moved in together.

Robin looked doubtful, but Lucas and I would just have to prove to him that we knew what we were doing.

When I took Robin to my apartment to pack up some clothes, all four of the other men accompanied us.

"Um," Robin said, gazing around at the bare floor and empty walls in confusion. "Where's all your stuff?"

"I should have warned you," I said. "When I was dealing with another situation a couple of weeks ago, someone tracked me back here and destroyed all my belongings looking for something." I had had to call a junk removal company to take everything away. I kept my clothes and toiletries in the apartment, but I had been sleeping on Steve and Baz's fold-out couch.

Steve snorted. "Not that he had much."

I shrugged and unzipped the suitcase I had borrowed from Steve. "Most of my personal items are in the house I own in northern California. Once we figure out where we will live permanently, I will move them."

It was not until I walked out of the closet with an armful of shirts and pants that I realized everyone was staring at me.

"What?"

Robin, whose mouth had been hanging open, said, "What do you mean, 'where we will live permanently'? We're moving?"

I looked at Robin, this young man—this *child*—who had dealt with so many traumas and changes in the last twenty-four hours alone, and I knew I had fucked up.

I dropped the clothes on top of the suitcase and strode over to him. "Not necessarily," I said. I put my hand on his arm. "Lucas does not want to live in Los Angeles anymore, but we have not had a chance to talk to you and Seth about where you might want to live."

Robin swallowed. "I, uh, like the house we're in now. Seth likes it too."

I cocked my head. I had not really considered us staying in George and Katrina's house permanently. We would have to build a wall around it to keep the paparazzi out, but some of the neighbors had them so that would not be an issue.

I said, "We will speak to Lucas about it tomorrow then."

There was a slightly awkward silence before Drake said, "So, Phillip, it sounds like you won't be using this apartment anymore."

I felt my eyebrows scrunch down. I really had not had enough sleep. "Yes, that seems to be the case."

He grinned. "Any chance you'd let me and Dirk sublet it from you? Baz is letting us take over his lease, but two of us in a one-bedroom is a little cramped."

"Oh. Ah. Yes, of course. I will speak to the apartment manager about what we need to do for that."

The twins fist-bumped each other.

"Damn, Phillip," Baz said. "We'll miss you around here."

I rolled my eyes. "The house we are staying in is 2.3 miles away. I am certain we will see each other again."

Steve said, "You know what every new family needs for a housewarming present?"

I gave him a flat stare. "We cannot have any rabbits because we have three dogs."

"Well, crusty cranberries, it was worth a shot."

CHAPTER 11
LUCAS

Phillip and Robin didn't get home until after 11pm. Phillip had sent texts updating me on their whereabouts, which was the only reason I hadn't freaked out.

Especially after I'd discovered the bottles of booze in the wooden sideboard in the dining room.

Seth had fallen asleep on the couch, cuddling the dogs, but I'd been restless in the unfamiliar place. I'd decided to explore.

I knew Phillip's friends had died, and from the brand-new bed in the primary bedroom, and the brand-new desk in the study, I was fairly confident they'd died in this house. That didn't bother me too much, but I wondered how Seth and Robin would feel about it if they knew.

I'd investigated the kitchen earlier in the day, so I started my exploration in the laundry room, which boasted expensive appliances, a sink, and cabinets full of table linens and laundry soap.

The dining room held only an oval table that could seat eight people, and a sideboard with barware on top. I'd known what

I would find when I opened the cabinet doors underneath, but I hadn't expected the quality of the alcohol. Top shelf and then some. Phillip's friends had lived large for sure.

I wanted to dump it all out in the sink, but I was worried about how the smell of all that alcohol would affect me. The last thing I needed was to sabotage my recovery while trying to aid it. I would have Phillip pour it out when he got home, I decided. Seth was in the house, and that fact more than anything helped me close the cabinet doors without hesitation.

I was poking through the books on the shelf in the study when I finally heard Phillip's SUV pull into the driveway. Relief flooded my body, and I didn't even feel embarrassed about it.

I went outside and saw a second SUV, a small Honda, park at the curb in front of the house. Phillip got out of his car with a small suitcase and a white paper bag that said, "Amy's Ice Cream" on it and walked over to where I was standing on the front porch in my socked feet.

"That is what I have been driving to work at the elementary school," he told me, indicating the Honda. "I gave it to Robin since he did not feel comfortable driving the Porsche SUV in the garage."

Robin hopped out of the car with a big grin. I couldn't help but return it. "How do you like the Honda?" I called to him.

"It's great!" he said as he trotted up the walkway. "It has heated seats and a sunroof!"

"Nice!" I looked over at the minivan. "Maybe we should return my rental and I can drive the Porsche."

Phillip nodded. "The titles have been transferred into my name so there will not be any issues with us using those cars. I will take the minivan to the car wash tomorrow before we return it. The outside is clean, but the inside needs attention."

I nodded. I would offer to help him, but odds were I'd be recognized. Hell, right now there was a chance Phillip might be recognized too.

"Seth fell asleep during the movie," I told them. "I, uh, wasn't sure if he'd react badly to me trying to wake him up, so I just left him there."

"Probably a good idea," Robin said. "I'll move him to his bedroom." He hesitated. "Seth has never slept by himself. He took a nap in there this afternoon, but if he's uncomfortable alone in the dark I'll stay in there with him."

Phillip said, "We should get him a night light."

I scoffed. "Night lights are boring. We should get him some glow-in-the-dark stars and put them all over the walls and ceiling."

"Does that mean we're staying here?" Robin asked, his tone eager.

"Uhhh...." I looked desperately at Phillip, who only raised an eyebrow at me, which was no help. "I guess we should talk about that, huh?"

Phillip finally intervened. "We can have a family discussion about it tomorrow when Seth can participate."

"Sure," I said with relief. That would give Phillip and me time to talk about it beforehand and be on the same page.

We went inside and Robin woke Seth up. I took note of how he started calling Seth's name from across the room so that Seth was mostly awake by the time Robin helped him off the couch.

I needed to find the kids a therapist ASAP. Hell, I needed one too.

So it'd be a good idea if we all knew where we'd be living.

Would it be so bad to stay here? Robin had sounded like he wanted to. What did Phillip think?

Phillip put his arm around my waist. "Come on, bedtime."

I let him guide me to our bedroom—*our* bedroom. What a mindfuck these last couple of days had been.

Phillip unpacked his clothes from the suitcase. He said, "I will have to get the rest of my clothes out of my apartment soon—one of my friends will be subletting from me."

I dropped my pants, stepped out of them, and tossed them into the hamper. "How do you feel about staying here? I figure your friends passed away in the house."

He winced. "That part is not easy, you are right. But I do not mind. The boys make the place feel different, happier." He walked up to me and tugged at my shirt. I lifted my arms so he could pull it over my head. "The question we need to settle first is whether you want to live in Bent Oak or pick somewhere else."

He tossed my shirt after my pants, and I was standing there in my boring cotton boxer briefs while he was fully dressed. This would not do.

I reached for the hem of his shirt but stopped before touching. "Is this okay?" He nodded, so I pulled his black t-shirt over his head like he had done for me. When he moved for the button on his pants, I smacked his hand away. He looked amused but held his hands out to the side.

I unbuttoned his suit pants and pushed them down by caressing my hands over his ass. I didn't think I'd ever get my fill of that ass in those silk boxers.

"Do *you* want to stay in Bent Oak?" I asked him as he stepped out of the pool of fabric at his feet. His boxers didn't hide anything. Damn, that was enticing. I started to chub up. No sex, I reminded myself.

"If you do not have a preference to move elsewhere, then yes, I would like to stay here. I have friends here, and I believe Robin at least is worried about moving."

This stopped me in my tracks.

"Worried? Do you think it's fear of the unknown, or what?"

Phillip frowned slightly. "I am not sure exactly. It might just be that the boys have had a lot happen to them in the past couple of days. We should probably talk to a therapist before introducing another big stressor like moving out of town."

"Okay. Let's just live here then." I left my arms by my sides but I moved closer so I was almost close enough to brush our cocks together. He was half-hard as well, and I noticed I was exactly the right amount taller than him to put his cock in a prime position. I put my mouth up against Phillip's, but I didn't kiss him. "I don't expect you to have sex with me tonight, but when you're ready, I want to be naked while you shove your silk-covered cock into my balls. Just putting my request in."

I felt his lips, still resting against mine, curve into a smile. "I see we have finished talking about moving."

"We have." I was about to step back when Phillip's arms came around me and his lips crashed into mine. I reveled in the sensations from his hot mouth and his talented tongue, not to mention his bare chest and his hands on my back. I tilted my hips away from his and fought mightily against the urge to put my hands on his silk-clad ass and slam us together.

But the kiss went on and on, and even without friction my cock was weeping into my underwear, and my balls were trying to climb into my body.

With a groan I tore my mouth from Phillip's. "We have to stop," I panted. "I'm about to come all over myself." I couldn't keep my hands from running over his shoulders.

Phillip looked intrigued. "I would be open to seeing that."

"What?"

He hesitated, then said, "I am not ready for sex. But," he gestured between us. "I am certain both of us need to come after this."

My cock twitched, and his lips quirked up.

"I'm listening," I said.

He pointed at the bed. "What if we watch each other get ourselves off?"

I nodded enthusiastically. "Yes. Let's. I'm in."

Phillip smiled and put his thumbs in the waistband of his silk boxers, and I cried out, "Wait!"

He stilled. "What's wrong?"

"Can I make another request? This one is for right now."

His head tilted to the side and he studied me with his dark eyes. "Of course."

"Can I use your boxers to jack off with?"

His eyes burned and his nostrils flared. "Fuck yes."

He slowly stretched the waistband out and lowered it to expose his cock. I licked my lips. It was perfect, thick and maybe a hair longer than I was comfortable deep-throating. The head was purple, straining out of the foreskin with a steady trickle of precum coating the length of his shaft before it pooled into the dark curls at his base.

I put my hand inside my underwear and gave myself one firm stroke. The friction, after my cock had been denied any for so long, sent shivers through my body.

Phillip slid the silk boxers down his legs. "Take off your underwear and get on the bed," he said.

I practically leaped to obey. I shoved the covers to the floor and, after I'd shucked off my boxer briefs, I sat on the side of the bed where I had napped, my legs spread and knees bent. I fondled my balls as I waited for Phillip to join me.

He picked up the silk boxers and climbed onto the bed. After arranging some pillows to support his back, he leaned against the headboard. Then he stared into my eyes as he took his boxers in his hand and stroked himself with them. "Like this?" he asked.

My cock jerked. "Oh, fuck. Yes, please." I spread my legs wider.

Phillip held the boxers out to me, and I took them reverently, careful not to touch his fingers. I didn't want him to think I was trying to push him into something he wasn't ready for.

I brought the boxers to my nose and closed my eyes as I took in Phillip's heady scent. He groaned, and I looked to see him mirroring my pose, but with one hand on his balls and the other at his nipple.

"Fuck, Phillip. I need to come." I took the boxers and cupped my balls with the silk. The cool material was decadent against my swollen sac. I couldn't decide where to look. I wanted to memorize the sight of Phillip thrusting into one hand while arching his chest into the other as his fingers twisted. But if I looked down, I could watch the dark blue silk sliding along my purpled shaft and stained with my precum.

Phillip cried out, "Lucas. Coming!"

I tightened my grip and pushed my cock through the silk one more time as Phillip's cock pulsed and his cum spurted. My entire body bowed with my orgasm, and I made an inarticulate sound before collapsing against the mattress.

"Holy hell," I panted, pulling the cum-soaked boxers off my flaccid cock. "Um, I hope these can be washed."

He laughed. "They can. They just need to be laundered separately with a special detergent." He leaned over the side of the bed and picked his t-shirt off the floor before wiping himself down with it.

I flopped myself around until my head was on the pillow next to Phillip's. He slid his body down to lie flat and turned on his side to face me.

I said, "I think it's safe to say that was hot as hell. Was it okay for you? Not too much?"

He smiled and scooted toward me, giving me a soft kiss when he was close enough. "I loved it. It was exactly what I needed, thank you."

“Good.” I closed my eyes and barely registered Phillip getting out of bed. I felt the sheet and blanket spread across me, and then I was out.

The next morning Phillip had all of us dressed and out of the house before 9am. We still didn’t have any groceries, so we stopped for breakfast, eating inside this time. No one seemed to recognize us, but I was wearing a ball cap and my fake glasses.

Then we all endured hours of tedious shopping. After we set up their new bank accounts, Seth and Robin both got phones, tablets, and laptops. Phillip had a locked compartment in the back of his SUV, which was handy for securing our tech purchases while we went into another store to buy the boys some clothes. We outfitted Seth and Robin from head to feet, and Phillip insisted I needed a heavier jacket as well.

We were on our way home at last when my agent called.

“Hey, Felicia,” I said warily. We’d just spoken yesterday evening. What new paparazzi hell was I in for now?

“Lucas,” she said in her *you’d-better-be-paying-attention* tone. “The superhero movie. The director wants to hire you for the role, but Michael Evanson wants to meet with you first.

I sat up in my seat. Phillip threw me a concerned glance before paying attention to the road again.

“Did he say why?” Michael Evanson was the producer in charge of the yet-to-be-named superhero blockbuster I’d auditioned for a few months ago. Last month their first-choice actor had dropped out of the film, and Felicia had been low-key optimistic that I'd had a chance at it. One of the many reasons I'd gone into rehab.

"He's seen the stories about you and your new little family." Felicia's tone was both approving and sardonic at the same time. It was one of her many talents. "He likes that you've changed your lifestyle, but he wants to meet with you in person to—I'm quoting here—'get a better sense of your commitment to sobriety and family life'." I could feel her eye roll through the phone.

I tried to keep my excitement under control. "In other words, he's another entitled prick—" I grimaced and mouthed *sorry* at Seth. "—who wants to see me jump through hoops so he feels like I've bowed to his magnificence before he'll give me the role. When does he want to meet?"

She sighed. "Lucas, I'm going to be honest here. I'm not sure meeting with him is the best idea. When he was talking about your commitment to your sobriety, I'm worried he's going to try to test you."

I narrowed my eyes at the road ahead. "What do you mean?"

She said grimly, "He's throwing a big New Year's Eve party at his house, and he wants you to attend. With your boyfriend. He'll only meet with you there and then."

I groaned. I knew exactly what those parties were like. Hell, at one time I'd sought them out. See and be seen first and foremost. Almost as important was bonding with powerful entertainment industry players over booze, drugs, and sex.

"You think he's going to try to hand me drugs and alcohol to see if I'll relapse?"

"I'm not sure, but I wouldn't eat or drink anything while I was there if I were you."

I looked over at Phillip, who was scowling as he listened to my side of the conversation.

"Thanks, Felicia. Send me the details. I can do this. Phillip will watch my back."

CHAPTER 12
PHILLIP

It was taking everything I had not to order Lucas to not go to that party.

As if he would listen to me. I would have to lock him up somewhere to keep him from going. And then he would never speak to me again.

Which was why I agreed to act as Lucas' unofficial bodyguard at that damn party. I was not interested in a future where Lucas and I were not on speaking terms. Kissing terms. Probably fucking terms.

After Lucas finished the call with his agent, he said to me. "Looks like I need to go to LA for New Year's Eve. Will you go with me?"

"Of course. Robin and Seth, do you want to accompany us?"

That had started the Great Travel Debate, which had lasted for the next hour, though it had felt like an eternity. At last, it was decided that, because the puppies were too young to stay somewhere like a pet resort and we did not know a pet sitter that we trusted—even though I had assured Seth that I could find one that came highly recommended—Robin and Seth would stay behind. Lucas and I would fly out New Year's Eve morning and return the following evening.

We had a light dinner—takeout again—before Robin and Seth settled in front of the TV with a video game, which allowed Lucas and me to retire to the bedroom to have the *discussion* I had been dying to have since he had hung up the phone earlier.

I had coached myself to be constructive in my comments. Lucas wanted this role, and people in the movie industry were capricious assholes on power trips. He had experience dealing with them, and he would continue to have to deal with them his entire career. I would have to let him handle those douchebags himself.

But at least he had said I would be going to that damn party with him.

Lucas entered the bedroom first. As I shut the door, he spun around and pressed me back against it. I allowed this, curious to see what he was intending. He gave me a firm kiss, then put his hand over my mouth.

"Phillip, I know you have a lot you want to say about this party, but you realize it's my decision to go, right? You can nod." I nodded, amused. He went on. "However, I know what those parties are like, and I'd appreciate having you with me to get me out of there if it ends up being too much."

He stopped speaking, and I waited. He gingerly lifted his hand from my mouth.

I started with, "There is no question. Of course I will go with you."

He relaxed slightly. "Good. Thanks."

"But I want to have Ripley run a background check on Michael Evanson before we go."

"Absolutely not."

"Lucas—"

"No. This is my job, not yours."

We glared at each other. But eventually I sighed and said, "Fine. You are the one playing this asshole's little game. I just wanted to give you an advantage." Before he could smile in victory, I said, "But if you go through all this, and he does not give you the role, then he is fair game. Agreed?"

Lucas laughed then kissed me. "Agreed."

Lucas had deemed my one remaining suit "not fashionable enough" to wear to a Hollywood New Year's Eve party. He seemed concerned that the other guests would assume I was his bodyguard instead of his romantic partner. I did not see the problem with this.

Not trusting any clothiers in the Austin area, Lucas measured me himself—with many apologies for putting his hands on me, though his erection told me he was not sorry at all. Then he sent my information to someone named Manuelo, who had promised to produce a suitable outfit.

Well, it could not be worse than the beaver onesie.

I had been concerned that Seth and Robin would be uneasy in the house without us, but neither of them were particularly clingy when Lucas and I were ready to leave for the airport. Even though it was early in the morning, the temperatures were in the sixties already. Seth was in the back yard playing some sort of chase game with Peppermint and Buddy while Holly relaxed on the deck in the sun.

When he saw us, Seth galloped over and threw his arms around Lucas and me at the same time. "Bye!" he shouted. I had never seen this level of physical energy from him at school. Perhaps removing the stress of living with Shackleford, combined with regular meals, was allowing a different side of him to come out.

I kissed Seth on the top of his head, and Lucas aimed for his cheek. We got one more hug before Seth was off to play with the puppies again.

Robin was sitting on a barstool at the kitchen counter, typing on his laptop. I frowned. "Robin, we need to get you a desk."

He gave me a shy smile. "Maybe for my bedroom. But I like being out here where I can see what's going on." His smile grew brighter. "And get snacks!" I smiled. We had finally ordered groceries, and Robin had permission to get pizza delivered for dinner tonight.

Lucas went over and put an arm around Robin's shoulder. "Remember, call or text us if you need anything. It doesn't matter what we're doing, we'll answer."

He got an eye roll. "I've been looking after me and Seth for years. We'll be fine."

I stifled a growl. They were out of that living situation now.

I said, "Can I hug you?"

He shrugged, but I got another little smile. "Sure."

Not wanting to press my luck, I gave him the same kind of hug Lucas had. He did not reciprocate, but he leaned into me, which I took as a win.

Lucas and I rolled our suitcases—well, I was still using Steve's, with his permission—out to the minivan, which the rental agency was allowing us to return at the airport. Robin and Seth would pick us up tomorrow night.

As we pulled out of the driveway, Lucas said, "Was it just me, or did our departure seem a little... anticlimactic?"

I barked out a laugh. "Yes, I was expecting at least Seth to exhibit some sort of separation anxiety."

"Maybe this is a good sign?"

"Maybe." Then I remembered something. "My neighbor from the apartment, Baz? His sister does family therapy. I am going to contact her next week for a referral." I hesitated. "I hope Seth can avoid talking about how Shackleford died."

Lucas glanced over at me. "I don't think his trauma is related to Shackleford's death, but we can ask him if that's something he thinks he needs to talk about."

I nodded. Though right now Seth might not think he needed to talk about anything at all.

I had been interested to see how Lucas and I traveled together. Nothing brought out people's interpersonal issues quite like dealing with the delays and petty inconveniences of airline travel. However, I was pleased that Lucas was just as easy-going at the airport and on the plane as he was in everyday life.

Over the past few days, I had felt myself getting more and more comfortable with Lucas, and more and more attracted to him. I was ready to be physically intimate, and being at Lucas' condo was a prime opportunity for us to have sex together for the first time without worrying about the boys being right down the hall.

Therefore I was hoping we would not have to stay at the party very long. Though it was New Year's Eve, so if Lucas felt some social pressure to stay until midnight, at least I would get a kiss out of it.

We took an Uber from LAX straight to meet with Manuelo, who was apparently open on Saturdays, at least for Lucas. We dragged our suitcases with us through a discreet wooden door on a quiet side street just outside of Beverly Hills. The small sign said merely, "Clothier".

Inside, the place screamed *expensive.* We walked into a showroom. Thick carpet on the floor created a hushed atmosphere that the ambient classical music only reinforced. Around the perimeter were mannequins in various outfits that seemed cut for the male body type but not all of them were traditionally male garments. Silk tuxedos, suits with skirts, slim linen trousers with a flowy top, some sort of Avant Garde boxy creation. Manuelo was very talented, though I was becoming extremely curious about what kind of outfit Lucas had picked out for me.

A tall, thin man wearing a lavender silk suit walked toward Lucas with both hands outstretched. "Lucas, darling, it's so good to see you." Lucas took Manuelo's hands and gave him an honest-to-god air kiss.

Then I was introduced, and Manuelo required an air kiss of me as well. When in LA and all that.

Then Manuelo said, "Come back to the fitting room. I'm assuming you're going to see Lafitte after this?"

Lucas smiled and said, "We are." This was news to me. I hoped Lafitte, whoever that was, offered lunch.

Manuelo sighed in relief. "I'm so glad. Because, darling, that hair and beard are crying out for help."

Lucas laughed. I didn't.

"Okay, then after we see how everything fits, you can go do that while I take care of the alterations. Then you can pick the suits up when you're done."

At least Manuelo was efficient.

We were directed to changing rooms, and mine had a white tuxedo hanging next to the mirror. The vest was electric blue with white threads running through it. A tiny white silk jock was laid out on a small dresser, along with a white bow tie, and onyx cufflinks. Black shoes with a high shine had been placed on the floor under the suit.

With a suppressed sigh, I disrobed completely. The white shirt and pants were cut very slim, but they fit well, and I still had a decent range of motion. But when I lifted the vest off the hanger, I saw a problem.

"Lucas?" I called.

"Yes?"

I heard him leave his dressing room, so I opened my door. I took a moment to admire him in his white pants and shirt. Apparently we were going to match.

I held up the problematic garment. "This is a corset."

Lucas looked at the corset, then he looked at me. His eyes blazed. "Put it on," he rasped.

"No sex in the dressing rooms!" Manuelo caroled from somewhere in the shop.

Somewhat reluctantly I allowed Lucas to put the corset on me. I buttoned up the front, and he tightened the laces in the back.

"Not too tight," I cautioned. "I need to be able to move."

"How's that?" he asked, stepping back to admire me.

I moved my arms and torso. I mean, I would have preferred to wear just a shirt, but it was not the worst thing I had ever worn —*cough*, beaver onesie, *cough*.

I looked up at Lucas. He was staring at me like he wanted to devour me. "Look," he mostly whispered. He pointed at the large, paneled mirror that arced around a small pedestal. I moved to get a better view.

"Oh, fuck." Okay, I was sold on the corset. Honestly, I had been sold as soon as I saw the look in Lucas' eyes, but now I understood.

I whirled on him. "Do you have one too?"

He nodded and sprinted back into his dressing room. I turned to the mirror again, pivoting from one side to the other. I knew my body was in good shape, and men had admired my ass for most of my adult life. But, hell.

My shoulders appeared impossibly broad. The corset prevented my shirt from hiding any of my shape as my body narrowed toward my hips. Which meant my ass popped out like a peach.

Lucas came out of his dressing room, buttoning the front of his bright gold corset. I would not have ordinarily picked that color for him, but it worked against the white.

"Turn around," I told him.

I picked up the laces and pulled them taut. Watching the corset tighten around his waist was more erotic than I had been prepared for. "Shit," I gasped. Quickly I tied off the laces, inserting my fingers between the corset and his shirt to make sure he had room to breathe.

Then I moved around to his front so I could look.

"Holy hell."

Lucas had been eating better these past few days, but he still was not up to what he had told me was his normal weight. But with the corset he no longer looked gaunt. He looked lean and sexy, like a cheetah instead of an underfed housecat.

"I told you I could distract people from how skinny you've gotten," Manuelo said as he came into the room with a wooden box containing a measuring tape, pins, and other items necessary to his trade.

Even though I had just been admiring the exact effect Manuelo was talking about, I bristled at the implied criticism of Lucas' weight.

Lucas must have felt me tense up, because he rested his hand on my back and said, "Let's go get your jacket so Manuelo can check the fit."

I felt better when Lucas followed me into the dressing room, spun me around, and kissed me. He pulled back too soon, and I chased his mouth with mine.

He cupped his hand on my cheek. "Time for that later. We have a lot to do today."

"Fine," I huffed. Then I leaned forward and said quietly into his ear, "After the party I want to see you in that corset and nothing else. And then I will slowly peel it off before making love to you."

Lucas' breath caught. He jerked his head back and his eyes searched mine. "Yeah?"

I smiled, slow and predatory. "Oh, yeah."

"Remember, no sex in the dressing rooms!" Manuelo called out.

CHAPTER 13
PHILLIP

MANUELO ONLY TOOK THIRTY MINUTES TO MARK our clothes and send us back to change. He was kind enough to let us leave our luggage with him while we went to get Lucas' hair and beard trimmed.

Lafitte turned out to be a woman with a prominent Adam's apple and the shoulders of a linebacker, but she had a gentle, calming air about her. She conferred with Lucas about what he wanted and then got to work right away, without any extraneous chitchat. I sat in a chair where I could watch, and Lucas threw winks my way every so often.

When Lafitte was done with him, Lucas looked like he could walk the runway at a Paris fashion show. His long-on-top hair flopped just so over his forehead. The beard that had been getting a little shaggy had been carved down to a heavy stubble.

I looked forward to seeing him in his corset. Maybe after the party we could both model our corsets for each other without anything else on. Though the silk jock I had been given was intriguing. Maybe Lucas had one too.

Thankfully Lucas fed me before we picked up our suits and our luggage from Manuelo. We checked in with the boys to make sure they did not need anything, then we had time for a short nap at Lucas' condo before we had to get ready for the party. Lucas' audience—sorry, meeting—with Evanson was at 9pm.

Lucas and I managed to only spend about ten minutes making out and running our hands all over each other in our corsets before we had to put on our tuxedo jackets and go downstairs to meet the car Lucas had arranged for the evening.

Our driver, Franklin, was strikingly handsome, probably an aspiring actor trying to pay his rent while he waited for his big break. I asked him to keep the car where he could come get us quickly, and he promised he would.

Michael Evanson's Beverly Hills mansion was enormous. Three stories and I was betting at least ten bedrooms. The lights along the drive and the walkway to the front door kept most of the house in shadow except for the windows. Every single room we could see was lit from within.

After exiting the car, Lucas and I got in line to have our names checked off the list. I was glad I had very reluctantly left my guns at home in Texas. Evanson had a security team with wands making sure no one was entering with any weapons.

"Lucas, my man! Where you been?" The late twenty-something guy in front of us in line greeted Lucas like a long-lost friend, but at least he did not try to hug him. The man wore sunglasses at night, a suit jacket with slightly oversized shoulders and no shirt underneath, two large gold necklaces, and an insincere smile.

Lucas went stiff, so I put my arm around his back and introduced myself in my best Texas drawl.

"Hey, there. My name's Phillip but seems like you bein' a friend of Lucas and all, you can call me Phil."

Lucas turned his head and blinked at me. Then he turned back to the guy with a brilliant smile. "This is my boyfriend Phil. Phil, this is Lil' Wiz."

Fortunately, the line moved forward then, and I did not have to utter the words "Lil' Wiz" in my Texas accent.

"What's up with the funny voice, there, *Phil*?" Lucas whispered in my ear.

After we were wanded and allowed to proceed to the door to the house, I said, "You did not like him. I introduced myself that way so if other people address me as 'Phil' then we will know they are possibly associates of his." I shrugged. "I did not have a particular reason for doing it, and it was probably unnecessary, but similar tactics have been useful to me in the past."

"Huh." Then he said, "Lil' Wiz used to have parties like this one. Lots of drugs. He isn't someone I want to be friendly with anymore."

We walked up the ostentatious front steps that led to the enormous double doors. They were propped open, spilling light and the sound of people talking and laughing out onto the stoop.

As we entered, several people turned to look at us, and then they promptly turned to each other and started whispering. Lovely.

The large foyer had a curved staircase on the right, and then the rest opened into a huge great room with floor-to-ceiling windows. The night was black on the other side of the glass, so I assumed we were not encouraged to tour the gardens.

Lucas did one pan of the room before catching my hand in his and pulling me toward the far side. I saw a bartender had been set up in the corner. When in doubt, get a drink to fit in.

"Lucas!" a woman's voice called from nearby.

We turned to see a slender redhead with short bangs and a sequin crop top over sheer pink palazzo pants. She looked vaguely familiar, but I could not place her.

Lucas grinned and dropped my hand to hug the woman. He kept one hand on her shoulder and put his other on my back.

"Phillip, this is Petra Schaeffer. She used to be my costar on *Heartbeat Hospital*. Petra, this is my boyfriend, Phillip."

"How do you do?" I said, with a nod of my head.

"Oh!" she said. "It's lovely to meet you. But I thought you were called Phil. Do you have a preference?"

Lucas dropped his hand from her shoulder.

I smiled genially and put a little Texas in my voice. "Phil is just fine." I rubbed Lucas' back and said to Petra, "We were just on our way to the bar, darlin'. Would you care to join us for a libation?"

"Oh!" she said. "Actually, could I borrow Lucas for a quick second? You could get drinks and by the time you get back I promise to return him."

She grabbed Lucas' hand and tugged on him to follow her. Uh, no.

I slid my arm around Lucas' waist. "Sorry, darlin'. Where he goes, I go." Lucas' eyes were slightly panicked, reinforcing my decision to stick close. I gave him a fond, patronizing smile. "Lucas and I don't have secrets from one another, so anything you say to him, you can say to me. Isn't that right, nugget?"

I hugged Lucas from the side, and he gripped my waist tightly. He withdrew his fingers from Petra's hand.

"How about I find you later, Petra?" he said. "I'm supposed to meet with Michael Evanson in a few minutes anyway."

She pouted and looked between us, her eyes calculating. "He hasn't made his appearance yet, but, sure. I'll catch you later." She gave a half-hearted wave and walked away.

Lucas looked slightly ill. "I don't know why, but I feel like I need to take a shower."

I gazed around the room, but no one seemed to be paying attention to us. Still, that interaction had been unsettling.

"How about some sparkling water instead?" I nodded in the direction of the bar.

He took a deep breath and said, "Okay."

Lucas kept a tight grip on my hand as we walked to the bar. A tall, somewhat muscular man was ahead of us waiting for his drinks. He gave us an up-nod as we drew close, then put a $5 bill in the tip jar before picking up two glasses of red wine.

The man made to walk past me but performed a poorly-executed fake stumble instead. His elbow collided with my chest, and one of the glasses of wine spilled all down the sleeve of my jacket.

"Oh, my god, I am so sorry!" the man said. He gazed in mock horror at the stain on my suit. I hoped for his sake he was not a professional actor. Swiftly he set his glasses back on the bar top. "Please, let me take you into the kitchen. I am certain Michael has some baking soda and we can get that stain out."

What the fuck was going on here?

I glanced at Lucas, who looked worried. “Sure,” I said. “That’s mighty nice of you. Lucas, maybe there’s a Coke in the fridge in there you can have.”

“Oh!” the man said. “I hate to take both of you away from the party.” He looked at Lucas. “Where are my manners? I’m Judson Hathaway.” Another TV actor. Great. Lucas and I introduced ourselves.

“Right.” Judson put his hand on my back. “Phil, you come with me, and Lucas can wait here for you. We’ll be right back.”

Before I could object, Lucas said, “Oh, no. I promised Manuelo I’d make sure Phil showed off his new suit all night. I think I should supervise the stain removal.” Having never dropped my hand, he just confidently walked in what appeared to be the direction of the kitchen. I followed along with a smile on my face. I should have made sure Ripley was available tonight.

Judson trailed behind us, wringing his hands.

When we got to the kitchen, Lucas shouted, “Coming through!” and wove through the crowd of caterers to the large double sink. He leaned against the counter and positioned me to stand between him and the room. Good. I was not about to allow us to be separated.

Lucas said, “Let’s take your jacket off.” He put his feet on either side of mine and used both of his hands to help me remove my jacket. The wine did not appear to have reached the corset, for which I was relieved. I had plans for the corset.

Judson appeared and said, “I’ll find the baking soda and be right back.”

I pulled out my phone and leaned into Lucas like I was showing him something. "I am contacting Ripley," I said quietly.

Lucas hooked one hand in the waistband of my pants. "Why the fuck do they want to get us separated?"

"I do not know, but I do not like it."

I pressed *Send* on my text to Ripley.

Me: *Urgent. Need intel on Michael Evanson, movie producer. At his party with Lucas. So far two not subtle attempts to separate us.*

Judson reappeared right as I got a reply. I handed my phone to Lucas so I could deal with Judson.

Lucas glanced at the phone and gave me a nod. He tucked the phone back into my pants pocket.

Judson, who moments ago had been so confident about baking soda being able to remove the red wine stain, was now acting uncertain.

He said, "Um, maybe if you could hold your jacket over the sink? I think I just need to sprinkle the baking soda on the stain, right?"

Holding my jacket over the sink would occupy both of my hands. The sink looked clean, if damp. I laid the jacket in the sink, stain up.

Judson sucked in a breath but gamely shook the box of baking soda over the jacket.

What the fuck could these people want with us? I did not see how I could be the target. My enemies were dead, and if I had missed someone, why would they wait until I was in LA to try for me?

Which left Lucas. What value did he have by himself? What threat were the two of us together that we were not when we were apart? Was this something to do with Lucas' sobriety? My mind filled with images of someone shooting him up with drugs against his will. But for what purpose?

And why had Evanson not just asked to meet with Lucas alone to discuss the movie role? I would not have thought twice about it.

One of the caterers, a short woman with a no-nonsense air about her, came over to see what Judson and I were doing. "Hon," she said to Judson. "That's not going to do the trick. Let me." She elbowed him aside and set about caking the baking soda on the stain. "There," she said. "We'll let that sit for about twenty minutes. My name's Valentina. I'll keep an eye on it if you want to come back and get it later."

"Thank you so much," I told her. Behind me I felt Lucas digging in his pocket to get his wallet out. Valentina accepted the $100 bill with a smile.

We thanked her again and, holding hands, Lucas and I left the kitchen. Judson had disappeared.

I checked my phone, but Ripley had not sent an update yet.

I pulled Lucas into a corner and put my arms around him. I hugged him to me so I could speak into his ear. "We have two options: leave or find Michael Evanson and get him to tell us what the hell is going on."

Lucas said, "I want to know what's happening. Screw the superhero role. I can have a long and happy life without it. But they're messing with you and me, and I need to know why."

I smiled into his neck. "Agreed."

I looked around. "I recommend starting upstairs. We will search the entire house until we find Evanson."

We had barely started for the stairs in the entryway when yelling began about twenty feet away from us. The crowd parted, creating a circle around a large man and a petite blonde woman. The man was handsome, probably in his forties. He had the look of someone who used to be an athlete but did not keep up with his workout regimen as much as he should have. The woman was much younger, maybe in her early twenties, though with Hollywood types it was hard to tell.

"I told you, we're done!" the woman shouted.

The man glanced at the crowd around them. He did not seem particularly interested in me and Lucas, but maybe he was a better actor than Judson or Petra.

He wrapped his enormous hand around the woman's rail-thin upper arm and said, "Let's go somewhere else and talk about it."

He started dragging her toward the front door.

"No!" She tried to peel his hand off her arm.

No one intervened, though a few people had their phones out to record everything.

"Phillip," Lucas said.

I grimaced. "I really do not want to leave you alone."

But the man had already pulled the woman halfway across the room.

"I'll stay right behind you, I promise."

I gave him a sharp nod, dropped his hand, and ran toward the couple.

I got in front of the man and pivoted, holding out a hand. "The lady said no, so let her go."

The woman tried to step toward me, but he stopped her with a brutal yank on her arm.

"She's not your concern," the guy said.

I looked at his hold on the woman's upper arm.

Meeting her eyes, I made a fist and wrapped my other hand around the wrist right below it. I held my arms up to show her. "Grab the wrist of the arm he is holding. See where his thumb meets his fingers? That is the weak point. Move your body in that direction and give your arm a good jerk at the same time." I demonstrated pulling my wrist.

"What?" the man said. But the woman did as I suggested, and with a shout she was free. I held out my arm and she got behind me, rubbing at her bicep where he had grabbed her. I maneuvered us to the side so the guy had a clear path to the front door. I wanted badly to look around for Lucas, but the man's eyes were squinting at me like he was considering throwing a punch.

"I think you should leave," I said.

Someone shouted, "The security guard is coming!"

I snorted to myself. A little late, but whatever.

My phone chimed, which I hoped meant Ripley had some information on Michael Evanson.

The man scowled at me and spat, "Bitch," at the woman before turning on his heel and leaving. Charming.

"Thank you so much," she said.

"No problem," I told her, but I was looking around for Lucas. I did not see him. My entire body went cold. "Where's Lucas?" I yelled, "Lucas!" Most of the partygoers either looked around and shook their heads, or they did not look at me at all.

Nonononono.

The woman said, "Do you mean Lucas McCord?" and I rounded on her.

"Yes. Did you see where he went?" Her upper arm was almost entirely red. Would someone allow themselves to be harmed like that in order to participate in whatever was going on?

She rubbed her arm. "Um, Michael told us this was an intervention."

"What?"

"Yeah, he, um, said you were abusing Lucas, and he wanted to get him away from you."

I blinked. "That is not true."

She said, "I hope not. I couldn't imagine you'd have helped me just now if so. Bart—" She waved in the direction of the guy who'd manhandled her. "He wasn't part of the script. He's my ex." She shook her head. "Long story. Anyway, I saw a couple of Michael's security guys take Lucas toward the kitchen."

"Thanks," I said. "And get a restraining order." I didn't wait for her reply.

The kitchen was, like before, full of catering staff, but no Lucas. I raced up to Valentina. "Did you see Lucas McCord come through here?" I asked her.

She shook her head. "I haven't seen anyone but our staff in a while. But there's an elevator down that little hall." She pointed at a hallway I had charged right by on my way to the kitchen.

I thanked her and ran for it.

There was nothing else in the hallway except the elevator door and a security camera. Evanson had to know I was coming for Lucas, and he had probably watched our every move since we had arrived.

I quickly evaluated my next step. I had no doubt Lucas would be on an upper floor by now, though there was the possibility this house had a basement.

The elevator would make me a target as the doors opened to let me out, but if—and this was a big if—no one was waiting with a gun pointed at me, I could mitigate the risk slightly by rushing out on the offensive. If I took the stairs I would have to run through the entire party, wasting time.

Fuck it. I pushed the button for the elevator.

I tried to control my breathing to get my heart rate down. I had never felt this anxious on an op. But I had never been personally involved with anyone on an op either. If Lucas was hurt, people were going to die.

I checked my phone.

RIPLEY

Nothing on facial recognition, but he could have had some work done. Looking into his background and finances. Seems a little too clean for someone that high up in the movie industry but I'm still digging

I did not recognize the man in the accompanying photo. He could have been between thirty and fifty years old. He had obviously had some wrinkles removed. His eyebrows were waxed into arches, and he had light brown hair around a receding hairline.

I put my phone back in my pocket as the elevator dinged. It had probably come from the third floor based on the time it took to arrive. That would be the place to start.

But the doors opened on two guys with their guns out, so none of my planning was worth shit.

CHAPTER 14
LUCAS

I STILL DIDN'T KNOW IF THE FIGHT BETWEEN THAT couple had been staged, but I'd been the one to encourage Phillip to help the woman, so there was no point in worrying about it now.

I had bigger problems.

Problems like the gun in my side and the two very large men who had forced me into this elevator.

The bigger one, who sported a flat-top crew cut I'd never expected to see on anyone not in the armed forces, pushed the button for the third floor. The smaller one—and by smaller I mean he only loomed over me by a couple of inches—prodded me with his gun and intoned, "No funny business."

Did he think I was capable of some sort of Captain America elevator takedown? Also, who said "funny business" these days? Had he been watching mobster movies?

If we got out of this alive, Phillip would be teaching me self-defense as soon as possible. Robin and Seth would probably like to learn too.

My heart squeezed at the thought of them. Phillip and I had to get back to our little family. Our home.

I knew he would come for me. I just hoped it wouldn't be too late.

The elevator doors opened, and I was shoved forward. The hallway had expensive-looking dark wood floors and about eight closed doors. I was brought to a halt at the third door on the right.

The bigger guy knocked.

"Enter."

I was once again pushed forward. Did they think I wasn't going to cooperate? The guns were kind of a big incentive.

I recognized Michael Evanson from seeing his picture in magazines and from being at the same parties over the years. We'd never spoken though, and this was probably the closest I'd ever been to the man.

He stood on the far side of the room next to a drinks cart, a glass of what looked like scotch in his hand. This was obviously his study, with a huge ego-boosting desk, a comfortable-looking seating area to the side, and framed posters of movies and TV shows on the walls.

Evanson looked between me and the men behind me, and he made a regretful face. "Mr. McCord, I deeply apologize that I had to resort to these methods to get you here alone. Please have a seat, and I will explain everything."

I didn't respond, but nevertheless I was prodded toward the guest chairs in front of the giant desk. At least it didn't sound like I was in immediate danger.

Which made me worry for Phillip.

Once I was seated, Evanson sat behind his desk and said to the men who'd brought me, "Thank you. Wait in the elevator for the other one and bring him here."

The shorter one said, "You got it, boss." He had definitely been watching mobster movies.

Evanson set his scotch down on the desk with his left hand. He was missing part of his pinkie and ring fingers. With his right hand he casually laid a very large gun on his desk. "I'm not intending to shoot you," he told me.

I swallowed and said, "Why the gun then? You asked to meet with me about the movie. I would have come up here on my own."

He winced. "I was concerned that the man you came here with would insist on coming as well, and I did not know how much influence he has over you. It was imperative to speak to you alone first."

"So this is about Phillip." How was Evanson even aware of Phillip?

He sighed and gazed at his glass of scotch, rubbing his thumb along the rim. Then he looked up. "The man pretending to be your boyfriend is not who he says he is, and he cannot be trusted."

"Oh?" I asked calmly. "So you've met him before? Is he some sort of enemy of yours? You manufactured an opportunity at a movie role for me in order to, what, lure him here?"

He shook his head. "I assure you the role is yours if you want it. But I saw the photo of you two and I knew he was using you to get to me."

I squinted at him. "Phillip is my nephew's third-grade teacher in a small town outside of Austin. I don't even have a part in your movie yet. How do you twist that into him trying to get to *you*?"

Evanson scoffed. "You were always our obvious second choice for the role after Westin Chesterfield. I would not have put it past Anglerfish to have pressured Westin to drop out of the movie."

"Anglerfish?"

Evanson leaned forward. "That's the code name for the man you know as Phillip Downs. He is a spy, a mercenary. Sometimes he works for governments, but not always. His specialty is long-term undercover operations that are so subtle the targets never suspect he might not be who he says he is. He could have easily found out you were next in line for the role. If we'd chosen someone else, he would have vanished from your life without a backward glance. Make no mistake, his feelings for you are not real, and he will throw you aside as soon as he achieves his mission."

I leaned back in the chair and crossed my arms. I remembered how Phillip had pushed to commit to a relationship. Someone as beautiful as he was could certainly do better than a rundown recovering addict like me. What if Evanson was right?

But then I remembered the look in Phillip's eyes. His affection for Seth and Robin, and his desire for me. No, Evanson was wrong. Phillip's feelings were genuine. Phillip would never have brought me here if he had known Evanson was dangerous.

I needed more information. "But if that's true, what does he want with you?" Then I thought of a more pressing question.

"And why are you telling me all this? Why not just kill Phillip? Or whatever his name is."

I went cold all over just thinking about it. Please let us be alive at the end of the night.

Evanson—which now that I thought about it probably wasn't his real name—spread his hands out wide. "I don't want to kill anyone, not even Anglerfish. I will give him an opportunity to tell me who hired him and see if he will agree to leave without bloodshed. He has a reputation as a man of his word. If he agrees to leave me in peace, I will do the same."

A knock sounded at the door. I sat up in my chair. Did they have Phillip? I hoped he wasn't injured.

"And as far as why I told you all this," Evanson said, picking up the gun. "I think you deserve to know exactly who Anglerfish is and why he is using you."

Evanson made a sad sound. "I am very sorry for this next part, but I'm gambling that he won't want you hurt. So in order for Anglerfish and I to have a civilized conversation, I'm afraid I have to hold you at gunpoint. I do hope this won't have a negative impact on our future working relationship."

My mouth dropped open. What the fuck?

Evanson leveled the gun at my chest. "Enter," he called.

CHAPTER 15
PHILLIP

I TOOK IN THE ROOM AT A GLANCE. LUCAS APPEARED unhurt but Michael Evanson was standing behind the desk pointing a gun at him. Evanson would not live to see the New Year.

I quirked an eyebrow at Lucas, and he said, "I'm fine. Just pissed off."

I smiled, "I imagine that will get worse before it improves." I strolled forward as if I was not restraining myself from leaping over the desk and disarming that fucker. I needed to get him to tell us why he was doing all this first. Then I would kill him.

"Wait outside," Evanson told the men who had brought me here. They shut the door.

I stood next to Lucas' chair. I wanted to put my hands on him, but I needed them free in case I had to move quickly.

This was why I had never had a relationship before. My lover would have been a target. But I was retired now, and I was done putting off my own happiness. I would burn the world to the ground if it meant Lucas and I could just live our lives the way we wanted to.

And I would start with this motherfucker.

"Do I know you?" I asked Evanson.

He smiled. "So you're pretending you don't know who I am, Anglerfish. How quaint." My blood froze in my veins. This was someone from my past. But who? I had taken out everyone who might have held a grudge before I retired.

Evanson said, "Have a seat." He gestured toward the empty guest chair with his left hand, which was missing part of the ring and pinkie fingers.

I sucked in a breath. "Mikhail Ivanov. Code name Thresher. Official reports said you died in Belarus."

I had come up against Ivanov several times, both of us attempting to kill the other in order to reach our targets. He had had significant cosmetic surgery, and he had completely eliminated his Serbian accent.

Evanson/Ivanov inclined his head. "It took a lot of planning to pull off. But we're here to talk about you, Anglerfish, and what you want with me. Sit down." He pointed at the guest chair again. His gun never wavered from pointing at Lucas.

He thought I was here for him? Bemused, I sat down.

I said, "I thought you were dead. I do not have any agenda where you are concerned."

Evanson gave a dismissive jerk of his free hand. "Not likely. I knew you were coming for me as soon as I saw your picture with Lucas here. I worked too hard to get out of that life and make this new one for myself to allow you take it from me."

Ah. We were here because he was paranoid. *Hmmm.* I could still kill him, but he was a well-known figure in the entertainment industry, and cleaning up after his death would take more effort than I really wanted to spend. Not to mention Lucas might react poorly to seeing someone killed right in front of him. That would derail my plans to get naked with him tonight.

I would have to talk Evanson into letting us go.

I put both hands palm up toward him. "I retired last year. I understand exactly what you mean about having a new life. The only job I have been on since then was personal. I had to avenge the deaths of Morningstar and his wife."

This distracted Evanson. "Morningstar is dead? I had not heard. He was a worthy opponent when we were after the same target in Istanbul about ten years ago."

I nodded. "I remember that op." I made a face. "Unfortunately, a couple of months ago Morningstar got on the wrong side of Kostya Orlov. I took out his entire syndicate."

Evanson's eyebrows flew up. "Really? I would love to hear how that went down." Then he seemed to remember he thought I was here to kill him. He shook his head once and said, "Never mind. What I want to know is, who hired you and what will it take to make you go away?"

Inside I relaxed. If he wanted to negotiate my "going away" he was not planning on shooting me. I just needed to convince Evanson I was not a threat to him. Our old rivalry meant nothing now. I was angry about his scaring Lucas, but otherwise as long as he was not hurting anyone, he had nothing to worry about from me. More power to him for managing to get out of that life. I had had a difficult time retiring as well.

I glanced over at Lucas. He seemed tense but not panicking. I would have to reward him later.

I cocked my head at Evanson. "So that is why you did not just come to Texas and take me out with a sniper rifle. You wanted to know who hired me. But all this." I moved my hand in a circle to indicate the three of us. "It could have been done more privately back in Texas, or even at Lucas' condo here. Why go through all this trouble with getting your party guests involved?"

Evanson huffed. "In Texas you're living with Lucas' nephews. I'm not going to risk the children's safety. And I set up the intervention so when you disappear, people will be glad you are gone and rally around Lucas. He'll need the support."

Lucas scrunched his forehead. "Intervention?"

I rolled my eyes. "He told the party guests I was abusing you so they would help him get you alone."

"*What*?" he shouted. "That's ridiculous."

I put my hand on his arm to calm him. Lucas went silent, but he glared daggers at Evanson.

Evanson said, "Seeing you in that photo with Lucas and his nephews made me angry on Lucas' behalf." I could hear his homeland coming out a little bit in his voice. "I regret every time I had to hurt innocent people in order to carry out my missions, and I vowed I would never do it again. Since Lucas and I will be working together, I will not lie to him about why you vanished from his life."

I blinked. He thought I was using Lucas to get to him, but he wanted Lucas to know about it so he would not be blindsided by my leaving?

His logic was a bit twisted, but at the same time it was kind of sweet.

I turned to Lucas and smiled. "You got the part? Congratulations!"

Lucas regarded me with disbelief. "You're excited about me working on a movie produced by this guy?" He tilted his head in Evanson's direction. "He has a gun pointed at me, and he told everyone you were abusing me!"

I shrugged. "His heart is in the right place. He will just have to apologize and tell them it was a misunderstanding."

I looked at Evanson. "I promise you, I am retired. I am not working for anyone, and I am not after you. I am not with Lucas for a job; I want to build a life with him and his nephews. If you are not hurting anyone, I am not interested in interfering with your life. You have my word."

Evanson considered me for a moment, doubt warring with a desire to believe me. Then he sagged, relaxing his arm so the gun was no longer pointed at Lucas. He ejected the clip and placed it, along with the gun, on his desk.

"I am much relieved to hear that." He smiled benevolently at me and Lucas. "I think this calls for a drink in celebration!" Then his expression turned horrified and he said to Lucas, "But I can offer nonalcoholic options!"

After toasting to our mutual nonaggression with seltzer water and lime, Evanson escorted us downstairs and spent the next thirty minutes walking us around and explaining to his guests that the information he had received about our relationship had been wrong and he was happy to see us together.

Most of the party goers seemed relieved, particularly Jenna, the woman I had helped get away from her ex earlier. It turned out she had a part in the same superhero movie as Lucas.

I had texted an update to Ripley, and he said he would dig around further to make sure there were no rumors of Mikhail Ivanov still being alive.

I retrieved my tuxedo jacket—now damp but stain-free—from Valentina and gave her another tip for assisting me in finding Lucas.

Lucas and I left the party just before midnight, our arms around each other's waists. I was having trouble not being in physical contact with him. Knowing he had been taken earlier had been terrifying. I wanted to attach myself to him so he would never be out of my sight.

It was not healthy, but I could probably work through it in a day or so.

While we waited for Franklin to bring the car around, I said, "I meant to ask you, how was it being around all the alcohol, especially with all the stress with Evanson?"

"Honestly, worrying about what was happening kept me pretty distracted, so I didn't have a lot of cravings. But I don't know how I'll feel once the excitement wears off. I think I do want to find a support group or something."

Franklin pulled up and jumped out to open the rear door for us.

I put my hand on Lucas' lower back and urged him into the car ahead of me. "We will work on that next week," I told him.

Much to Franklin's amusement, Lucas and I had our first New Year's Eve kiss together in the backseat of the car going down the 101. We managed to keep our hands above our waists for Franklin's sake, but it was a struggle on my part.

When we reached Lucas' building, we rode up in the elevator with other tenants, which prevented any touching. By the time we opened the door to his condo, we were desperate for each other.

The front door closed. I tossed my tuxedo jacket to the floor and jerked my bow tie off. Lucas toed off his shoes while I took care of his tie. I got rid of my own shoes and socks, along with my pants. Our corsets had to come off so we could remove our shirts, but, eyes locked on each other, we both put the corsets back on. Once again, the sight of the material pulling snug around Lucas' waist sent heat through my body.

We stood in the middle of Lucas' living room, clothes scattered around us, wearing only our corsets and the silky white jocks, which were barely containing our erections.

I did not know what Lucas saw when he looked at me, but from my viewpoint, he was stunning. The shimmering gold corset drew my eye down to the brown curly hair peeking above the white silk at his groin. The white straps outlining his ass cheeks were perfection.

"I need you," I growled out, stalking toward him.

Lucas sucked in a breath and grabbed his dick through his jock. "I want you to fuck me. Bend me over and fuck into me with everything you've got."

"Yes." I reached for him, running my hands over the corset and down to his bare ass cheeks as our mouths met in a hot claiming kiss.

Lucas seemed obsessed with what I was wearing, brushing his fingers along the edges of my corset and sliding them beneath the straps of my jock.

I tore my mouth from his and licked down his neck. The fabric and buttons of our corsets caught as we moved against each other. It was time to feel Lucas' skin. I needed him bare in my arms, moving under me.

"We should move this somewhere else. Jump up," I said, leaning over to cup my hands under his naked thighs.

He laughed a little as he put his arms around my neck and sprang up. I staggered a bit, trying to find my balance as Lucas wrapped his thighs around my waist and crossed his calves over my ass.

I slowly let him slip lower until our silk-covered cocks were aligned, and his eyes rolled back in his head at the pleasure. He let his head fall onto my shoulder as I walked into the bedroom. The movement of my legs increased the pressure between our bodies and we both moaned.

Lucas humped against me. "Fuck, we need to do this as often as possible before I gain all that muscle weight for the role."

"Nugget, I'm going to work out right beside you just so I can keep holding you like this."

"Nugget? No. That nickname is not sexy. I thought you were using that at the party for your Texan persona."

I smiled. "I was, but I like it. Nugget."

He groaned but I distracted him by inching my fingers toward his hole. He tightened his arms and legs around me, arching his ass out.

I walked past the bed and into the ensuite bathroom. I told Lucas to take one of the towels off the rack, and then I leaned over so he could spread it out on the countertop next to the sink. I had to lift him slightly to set him down on the towel.

I stayed between his legs, my balls pressed against the cold edge of the countertop beneath the towel. Lucas' dick smeared precum on my corset through his soaking wet jock, but I did not care. I could easily remove the stain later with a mild detergent.

I watched in the mirror as I loosened Lucas' corset laces. The shiny gold fabric seemed to glow next to his skin. I laboriously undid each of the tiny buttons down his front, distracting Lucas by fucking his mouth with my tongue. When he was finally free of his corset, he writhed against me, moaning, his thighs moving restlessly along my hips and his trembling fingers tugging at my own corset laces.

He whined when he got to my buttons. I helped him, starting from the bottom so our hands could meet in the middle and make the task go faster.

When the buttons were free, I slid out of my corset before shoving my jock to the floor, kicking it somewhere behind me.

Lucas' hair was wild, his lips kiss-swollen, and his face red with beard burn. His eyes were half-lidded and sensual, and his lips kicked up at the corners as he took in my naked body. He plucked at my nipples, and the heat shot to my dick so intensely I thought I would come.

The stark white of the jock against Lucas' pale, pale skin had me moving forward, lifting him off the countertop. Once he was safely on his feet, I spun him around and my hand in the middle of his back and bending him face-down.

"God, yes, Phillip. Fuck me, please!" he cried out.

I put my hands between his thighs and nudged him to spread his legs further apart. When he was at a comfortable height, I rewarded him by shoving my hand into his jock from underneath. I fondled his balls with one hand and pulled down on his dick with the other. Lucas moaned and tried to rub his perineum against my forearms, but I pinned him against the countertop to keep him from moving. His face in the mirror was slack with pleasure, his mouth open to pant.

"Let me see your hole," I said. I pulled my hands out of his soaking wet jock and brought them up to spread his ass cheeks, tucking my fingers under the straps on either side.

I used my thumbs to open him up and spat into his hole. Lucas moaned and lifted his hips. I squeezed my hands, my thumbs pulling his rim even tauter.

Lucas shivered. "Phillip, please. I need you in me. Fuck me. Fuck me now."

I released my fingers from his cheeks, my dick jerking when I saw the red marks I had left. I shoved both thumbs at once into his hole, and he cried out, thrusting his hips back to take them deeper.

I could not wait any longer. I pulled my right thumb out, stuffing him with my left to soothe his need. I reached for my toiletry kit on the other side of the counter and pulled out the lube and condoms I had packed.

I tossed the condom to Lucas. "Open that, please."

"Yessss," he hissed, snatching it up and opening the wrapper.

I uncapped the lube one-handed before drizzling it down his crack. He humped against the thumb I was moving inside him, the straps of his jock framing his thighs and making me wish for a free hand to remind myself just how wet the fabric was against his dick.

I withdrew my thumb and replaced it instantly with my first two fingers.

Lucas whined, "Your cock, Phillip. I need your cock."

"You are not loose enough yet. Soon."

"No. I'm good. I want it so bad."

I slapped his ass cheek with my free hand, and he gasped. I met his eyes in the mirror, and they were dark with lust.

"Phillip, baby, I'm serious. I need you inside me right this fucking minute."

He tossed the unwrapped condom over his shoulder, and it slid down his sweat-damp spine to rest just above his crack.

"Fuck," I whispered.

I added a third finger to his hole while I suited up. Then I pulled my hand out, lined myself up, and pressed in.

"Oh, fuck," I gritted out. He was tight, so tight, but he moaned and pushed back to take more of me. I watched my shaft disappear inside his hole until my pubic hair was filling his crack. Fuck, I could look at that forever.

"Move," Lucas whimpered, bouncing on his toes to spur me on.

I pulled almost all the way out, then pressed back in, faster than before.

"Harder," he ordered, his voice lower, more guttural. He had his arms braced on the edge of the countertop and his head hung down. "Fuck me harder. Give it to me!"

I obeyed, using my hands to pull his hips into me while I thrust forward, then reversing both. Over and over, I rammed into Lucas' hole, his cries of, "Yes!" filling my ears. My entire world had narrowed to the feel of Lucas' heat around my dick, and where my hands gripped his body.

When I was on the edge, I reached one hand into his sopping wet jock and stroked him once. He bucked, wailing out his release. His dick pulsed in my hand, and his hole tightening around me. I slammed into him through my own orgasm until my thrusts slowed and I bowed over Lucas' back.

I kissed his shoulder and pulled my hand out of his jock, as I slid my dick from his hole. "You okay?"

Lucas grunted. Taking that for a yes, I dealt with the condom, then helped him stand upright. He leaned back into me.

I looked at him in the mirror, admiring his fucked-out expression and his sagging jock. I tugged it down and after Lucas stepped out of it, I kicked it to the side to be dealt with later.

I guided Lucas over to the shower and turned it on, ushering him inside once the water was warm enough. I gently cleaned him all over. When his eyes fell closed, and he leaned his head down so I could wash his hair, my heart felt almost too big for my chest.

When I was clean too, I shut the water off and kissed his cheek. He stood still while I toweled him dry. His hair was still damp, but he would be warm enough sleeping under the covers.

I debated asking him if he wanted underwear or sleep pants, but selfishly I needed his skin against mine, so I did not bring it up.

Lucas let me slide him between the sheets, then I followed and snuggled him against me. I nuzzled my nose into his shoulder. "Good night," I said.

"*Mmmm*. Love you," he mumbled.

I smiled so hard I could not get to sleep.

Which worked out well because my phone rang about thirty minutes later. Cursing myself for leaving our phones in our pants in the living room, I tossed back the covers and ran naked through the condo. I snatched up my pants and pulled my phone out of the pocket just as the ringing stopped.

Robin had called. Shit.

I called him back, snagging Lucas' phone out of his pants while I waited for the call to connect.

"Phillip?" Robin said.

"What is wrong?" I snapped, before wincing. "Sorry, I did not mean to bark at you."

"I'm sorry to call so late."

"I would rather you call than not, okay? What is going on?" I walked back into the bedroom. Lucas was sitting up, rubbing at his face. My chest squeezed with a combination of caring, affection, joy, and concern.

I put Robin on speaker just as he said, "Seth had a nightmare. He's worried you won't come back from your trip." He blew out a breath. "He also didn't want me to call you."

"You did the right thing, Robin," Lucas said. "We're always available for you guys, even if it's in the middle of the night."

"Okay. Um, let me go into Seth's room. I just came out to get my phone."

I sat down on the bed next to Lucas and put my arm around him. "We should go back first thing tomorrow instead of later," he whispered. "Packing up my condo can wait."

I nodded and kissed his temple. He unlocked his phone and opened the airline app.

"Hello?"

I put a smile in my voice. "Hey, Seth. We heard you had a bad dream."

"Hi, Uncle Phillip. I told Robin not to wake you. Um, is Uncle Lucas there too?"

"I'm here, buddy." He pressed a button on the app and gave me a thumbs up. "Hey, I'm glad you guys called. Phillip and I missed you and we decided to take an earlier flight home tomorrow. We'll get in around noon."

"Really?" The hope in Seth's voice almost broke my heart.

I cleared my throat and said, "Yes. Do you want us to take you out to lunch?"

"Yeah!"

We chatted with them about the New Year's Eve countdown show they had watched, and soon Robin said, "We're getting sleepy over here, so why don't we let you go, and we'll see you at the airport when you land?"

Lucas said, "Sure. We'll text you from the plane so you know we're on time."

"Okay. Um, thanks."

"Thank you, Robin," I said sincerely.

We hung up and I looked at Lucas. "Robin can choose for himself, but next time we travel, Seth is coming with us. At least until he knows we will not leave him."

Lucas put his arms around me and nodded against my neck. "That poor kid. Both of them. We also need to make sure Robin has at least a little bit of a normal childhood before he goes off to college."

"Yes. And that he does not feel like he has to parent Seth anymore."

He leaned his head against my chest. "Time to find a therapist."

"Yes."

He added, "And a lawyer, so I can get official guardianship."

I smiled. "You are going to be a great dad."

Lucas snorted. "*We* are going to be great dads. Don't think I didn't notice whose phone Robin called tonight."

I chuckled, then kissed his temple. I closed my eyes and leaned my head against his. "I never thought I would have a family. I will do everything in my power to be the best partner and the best father figure I can."

Lucas turned his head and put a hand to my face. I opened my eyes, and he said, "All you have to do is be yourself."

EPILOGUE

PHILLIP

A couple of weeks later we went to dinner with Cole Washburn and his two boyfriends, Will and Jason, at their ranch, which functioned as an animal rescue.

Also in attendance were my neighbors Steve and Baz, along with Steve's brothers Dirk and Drake.

Dirk had moved into my old apartment already, and we were set to complete the subletting paperwork with the apartment complex next week.

When we had first arrived, Cole and Steve had been in the middle of a discussion about something to do with the dating app Steve and his business partner were developing with Cole's funding. The rest of us had gone out on the back deck to talk and let Cole, Will, and Jason's dogs run around. Jason told us that once the puppies were weaned and vaccinated, we could bring them and Holly to play with Brooks and Reiner.

Will had taken Seth and Robin to see some horses and a couple of alpacas, and when they had returned, Seth was practically exploding with excitement about all the animals.

We had been served a wonderful meal of steaks and vegetables, with wine for the adults who wanted to partake. Lucas did not seem bothered by its presence. He and Cole fell into an extended conversation about muscle-building meal plans, and I was glad to see a friendship developing there.

Seth was ensconced in a recliner with his tablet and an orange cat on his lap while Robin, Dirk, and Drake were lined up on the couch playing a video game that involved an improbable number of guns. The three of them were about a year apart in age, and none of them had had an easy childhood, so I was happy to see them having fun and acting like kids.

Lucas and I had met with the family law attorney multiple times this week. We were waiting for a date to go before a judge to finalize Lucas' guardianship of the boys, but in the meantime he had been granted temporary custody.

I had returned to my substitute teaching job. Originally I had intended only to work the remainder of my three-month commitment, but the principal had offered me a full-time position. I had accepted a contract through the end of the spring semester only. In the fall Lucas would have to be on location filming his movie. We were waiting to see how Seth's therapy progressed before deciding whether he would be better off staying in Bent Oak with me and going to school in familiar surroundings, or if I would homeschool Seth while he and I joined Lucas wherever he was filming.

Robin had already enrolled in some online programming classes, and he was scheduled to take the GED in a few weeks. Lucas and I were encouraging him to apply to go to college on an actual campus, but we would let him make the final decision.

I looked around the room at my friends and family. After all those years of pretending to care about people only to kill them or steal from them, I never imagined I could have a life I loved this much.

I never imagined I could have someone like Lucas.

I watched him talking with the other men. His face was flushed from laughing.

Suddenly I wanted Lucas to know that I was all in, permanently. That he was my person forever. And I needed him to know it right that very second.

I stood up from my chair. All eyes turned to me. I said, "Lucas, would you join me out on the back deck for a moment?"

His forehead wrinkled, but he just said, "Sure," and got up from his chair.

Outside the January air was crisp but not uncomfortably cold. The sky was clear and without the light pollution from the city we could see a huge swath of the Milky Way. I could not have chosen a more romantic setting.

I embraced Lucas and leaned in to give him a kiss.

He smirked. "Is that why you brought me out here? I'm not shy. You could have done that in front of everyone else."

I smiled back at him and shook my head. I said, "New Year's Eve night, in your condo. When you were falling asleep, you expressed, uh, a certain level of affection for me."

He froze, and his smile dropped. "I did?"

I ran my hand down his arm and took his hand in mine,

holding it against my chest. "You did. And I want to be clear that I am well on my way to feeling the same."

His smile returned, and he put his other hand on my neck. "I'm glad to hear that."

"We already made a commitment to one another, but I find myself wanting more."

"More? What kind of more?"

"More commitment." Still keeping his hand in mine, I went down on one knee.

Lucas gasped.

From inside the house, I heard Dirk shout, "Holy shit, are you guys seeing this?"

I looked up into Lucas' beautiful eyes, the hazel darkened to brown in the dim light. "Will you marry me?"

His mouth moved but he did not get any sound out. Finally he said, "This is really fast."

"I know, but I am ready. I am also willing to wait if you are not. Or we can have a really long engagement. I promise you will not disappoint me, whatever your answer is."

"*Hmmm.*" He put the forefinger of his free hand on his chin like he was weighing the pros and cons. "It would look better for my guardianship of Seth and Robin if I could show you and I were together for the long haul."

I grinned. "That is true."

He looked up into the night as if seeking inspiration before his eyes returned to mine. "And then we could apply to officially adopt the boys together."

My breath caught. "I would love that."

From inside the house, Seth shouted, "Say yes, Uncle Lucas!"

But Lucas frowned and spun his finger around to point at me. "I don't want that hideously ginormous diamond ring you put in the safe in the study. I want us to pick out our own rings together."

I nodded. "That ring has bad connotations for me. I will get rid of it soon. Our rings will have happy connotations only."

He stared at me some more. My heart started to beat faster.

Not able to stand the wait any longer, I said, "So, will you marry me?"

His face broke into a huge grin. "Yes, I will!"

Cheers came from inside the house as I stood and kissed him.

Thank you for reading *We Don't Need Another Santa*! Curious about how Phillip met Steve and Baz, along with Dirk and Drake? Check out *What's Santa Got to Do with It*!

ALSO BY BIX BARROW

BENT OAK, TEXAS

Holding On to a Hero (Will, Cole, and Jason's story)

Heart Me Up (Craig and Foster's story)

Head Over Feels (Felix and Malcolm's story)

What's Santa Got to Do with It (Steve and Baz's story)

We Don't Need Another Santa (Phillip and Lucas' story)

I Touch Hoses (Keson and Wesley's story) – Related novella

Last Mango in Palm Springs (Ford and Zachary's story) - Related novella

Voices Harry (Mitchell and Harry's story) – Free when you go to www.bixbarrow.com and sign up for my newsletter!

WONDERFALL

Seer (Cal and Greg's story)

Medium (Shane, Ellis, and Rory's story)

Wonder (Simon and Reno's story)

SINGULAR MAGICS

Unprecedented (Manny's story)

LOVE IN MAPLEWOOD (MULTI-AUTHOR SHARED WORLD)

Can You Feel the Maple Tonight (Drake and Finn's story)

ABOUT BIX BARROW

When Bix Barrow got an idea for her first book, it ended up turning into her second — and thus the first two stories in the *Bent Oak, Texas* series emerged. An aspiring author for most of her life, it took a foray into the MM romance genre to spark the steamy scenes and blazing banter Bix now weaves into her novels. Accompanying her on her writing exploits are her two dogs and multitude of cats (six at last count). An avid traveler, Bix has started to view her expeditions as interviews for her future home. Born and raised in Texas, she is eager to move somewhere with fewer politicians, hurricanes, and flooding.

Join Bix Barrow's Boom Boom Room on Facebook for sneak peeks and fun conversation!

Sign up for Bix's newsletter and get a free novella! www.bixbarrow.com

facebook.com/bixbarrowauthor
instagram.com/bixbarrow
bookbub.com/authors/bix-barrow

www.ingramcontent.com/pod-product-compliance
Lightning Source LLC
Chambersburg PA
CBHW061237170626
46809CB00007B/2711

* 9 7 8 1 9 6 4 6 1 6 1 0 0 *